EXCHAN

In September 1983, Corgi Books, in conjunction with Central Television's Saturday Show (which is networked throughout the UK), launched a competition to look for an English cover girl for the title EXCHANGE OF HEARTS in the Sweet Dreams series.

The judges were Steve Strange, Tommy Boyd (presenter of The Saturday Show), the head of a London modelling agency, and two art directors.

Thousands of entries were received from all over England, and after a great deal of thought, the judges' choice was narrowed down to six finalists. A lunch was held in London in November, and the winner, pictured on the cover, was Anita Hoy, aged fourteen, from East Molesey in Surrey.

Exchange
of Hearts

Janet Quin-Harkin

BANTAM BOOKS
TORONTO · NEW YORK · LONDON · SYDNEY

RL 6, IL age 11 and up

EXCHANGE OF HEARTS
A Bantam Book / June 1984

ISBN 0-553-17875-X

Published simultaneously in the United States and Canada

*Bantam Books are published by Bantam Books, Inc. Its trademark,
consisting of the words "Bantam Books" and the portrayal of a
rooster, is Registered in U.S. Patent and Trademark Office and in
other countries. Marca Registrada. Bantam Books, Inc., 666 Fifth
Avenue, New York, New York 10103.*

Printed and bound in Great Britain by Hunt Barnard Printing Ltd.

O   0 9 8 7 6 5 4 3 2 1

For my goddaughter, Kate,
who gave me the idea

Chapter One

It happened on Tuesday, June 5, at 4:45 P.M. Until that moment it had been a perfectly normal day for Fiona Henley. School had been the normal mixture of boring and not so boring. They'd studied worms in biology, and Fiona had thought she was going to faint when one had wriggled toward her. Fiona had been chosen to sing a solo in the summer concert. They'd had sausages and chips for lunch. She'd walked most of the way home with her boyfriend, Simon, and promised to call him as soon as her homework was done. A very ordinary day.

The weather was ordinary, too, a heavy gray afternoon. The fine drizzle of rain, so often part of the English summer, settled on Fiona's fine blond hair like jewels. The world seemed to be made up of different shades of gray. Fiona's school uniform was gray, too, and she hated it.

She was not the sort of person who liked being told what to do, and she especially hated wearing a uniform. The school was strict about it, too, no colored hair ornaments, no colored shoes. *It's a wonder they don't dye our hair gray to match,* Fiona thought. Thank goodness for that. Fiona loved her beautiful blond hair. She pushed a loose lock back under her school hat and shifted her heavy schoolbag from one shoulder to the other as she turned for home.

At the corner a bright-red double-decker bus made a splash of color on the gray London street. It came to a halt, then roared off again, leaving its diesel smell behind. Fiona crossed the street, looking forward to a cozy evening in front of the telly. Her house was like all the others on the block, a dark red brick two-story, attached to its next-door neighbor. Only the front doors allowed any individual choice—some natural wood, some bright-colored paint. Fiona's own front door was frosted glass.

Fiona let herself in with her key and paused in the narrow front hallway to take off her damp school raincoat and hang up her hat. The house seemed quiet. *A bit late for tea,* she thought sadly. Her parents would have finished, and only some dry slices of cake and a lukewarm pot of tea would be left. Fiona was about to go in and greet them when she heard her name mentioned. She stopped short in the hallway and listened.

"It would do her the world of good." Her mother's pert English voice came from the sitting room. "She's already becoming much too set in her ways."

Her father's voice joined the conversation. "That's right. And much too serious about this Simon boy."

"Of course, I must admit it's been partly our fault, Humphry," her mother's voice came again. "We have tended to make things easy for her. We've probably protected her too much and spoiled her, too, but she is an only child—"

"So, she can go over in September?" her father interrupted.

"I think that would be fine. She'd just catch the beginning of the school year, and she could stay until summer vacation," said a deep, drawling, American-accented voice. That was Professor West. He was a visiting lecturer at London University, where her father taught, and he'd been renting the upstairs flat from them all year. Fiona's curiosity got the better of her. She walked into the room, trying to look as if she hadn't been listening in on the conversation.

"Oh, hello, Mummy, hello, Daddy, any tea left for me? I'm positively starving," she said brightly. "Hello, Professor West."

Her parents were still sitting at the table: her mother, a petite woman who often reminded Fiona of a chirpy sparrow, and her serious-looking father, who peacefully ignored his wife's

3

excited chatter. Professor West was sprawled out in the armchair by the empty fireplace. His long legs stuck out across the hearth rug. Fiona had thought her father was tall until she met Professor West. She had been rather scared of this enormous man at first, but over the year she had seen that he was quiet and gentle.

"Hello, darling, we were just talking about you," her mother said.

"It's not nice to talk about people behind their backs," Fiona quipped and helped herself to a piece of cake. "That's what you always tell me."

"Well, this is rather special," her mother went on. "We have been making some splendid plans for you."

"Plans for me? You mean for the summer holidays?"

"No, darling, for next year at school."

"You mean I'm going to a new school next year? What's wrong with the one I go to now?"

"Nothing, dear, but a wonderful opportunity has come up for you," her mother said breathlessly, flushing a little.

"Fiona," Professor West interrupted, "I've just suggested to your parents that you and my daughter Sherry do an exchange next year. She'd come to London, and you'd live with us in New Mexico. How does that sound to you?"

Fiona opened her mouth, but no sound came out. She was trying desperately to remember where New Mexico was on the map and if it had

4

anything to do with old Mexico and if they had tornadoes.

"It will be wonderful for you, dear," her mother added. "What an opportunity, to live in a different country, to go to a different sort of school. This is a chance not many girls have."

Fiona forced her jaws to move. "Let me get this right," she said slowly. "You want to send me to America for a whole year?"

"That's right," her mother said, nodding her head in encouragement.

Fiona looked from her mother to her father to Professor West. Then she shook her head. Thoughts of Simon and the school choir and exams she had to pass were all flying around inside her head. "Oh, no," she said, "not for a whole year. I couldn't possibly." Then she rushed out of the room.

Upstairs in her room Fiona lay on her bed and stared at the rose pattern of the wallpaper. On one wall hung a large oval, gilt-framed mirror. It had been Fiona's grandmother's, as had the chest of drawers and the dressing table. In fact, almost every item in the room had a history. She tried to imagine a whole year without seeing them, but she couldn't. They were just too much a part of her life. All the future she had taken for granted—her next year at school, the solo with the choir, Simon's living right around the corner—how could she survive a year without these things?

New Mexico! Fiona lay and thought about it; she tried to think unemotionally. She knew that Professor West came from America, but she'd never bothered to find out much about it, and now it seemed as remote as the moon. Wasn't New Mexico close to the border with old Mexico, and didn't they have bandit raids and other equally unsafe and undesirable things? *I don't care where it is because I know I don't want to go,* she thought angrily.

She was still staring at the wallpaper when her mother crept in and sat on the end of her bed. Fiona grunted a hello to her.

"I know this is a big deal, darling," her mother began. "Perhaps we broke the news a little too quickly."

"Perhaps you should have thought to ask me before you arranged everything," Fiona said, still staring at the roses. "After all, it is my life you are messing about with."

"Don't put it like that, darling," her mother said, sounding hurt. "You make it sound as if it's a punishment, not a wonderful chance for you."

"I don't think it's a wonderful chance at all," Fiona said, still not looking at her mother. "It's just ruining my life, that's all. When I get back, I shall be behind everybody in school, I shall do badly in my exams, they will have found somebody else to sing the solos in the choir, and Simon will have found a new girlfriend. And what will I have got out of New Mexico, for heaven's sake? Maybe I'll have learned to speak with a funny American accent."

"Fiona, don't be so silly," her mother said angrily. "Living in a different culture is a wonderful experience. You are growing up in a very protected little world here: you have Daddy and me to look after you; you have Simon to walk you home from school. If you don't have new experiences, try new things, and travel to new places, you'll never find out that other worlds exist. I understand you're frightened. I would be, too, if I were going away for the first time."

Fiona was quite used to getting around her mother and usually managed to get her own way in the end. She decided to try a different approach. "But, Mummy, you know how shy I am. I really don't do well with new people. They'll all laugh at my accent, and I'll feel an utter fool." She got up and slithered across the pink eiderdown to her mother, snuggling against her. "Don't make me go, Mummy, please! I promise I'll go away to university when the time comes and I won't make a fuss, but not now. Don't send me all the way to America. I don't think I can bear to be a whole year without you."

"Of course we won't *make* you go, darling," her mother said. "Your father and I would never force you into anything you were completely

7

against. But I do know that if you turn down a chance like this, you may regret it for the rest of your life. It won't be easy for you, I know that. And it won't be easy for Daddy and me to do without our little girl for a year."

"Don't send me then," Fiona pleaded. "I don't want to be miserable as well."

Fiona's mother, beginning to realize she was being manipulated, said airily, "Oh, don't worry about us, darling. We are willing to make the sacrifice for you." Then she slid from Fiona's grip, gave her daughter a little kiss on the forehead, and went out, closing the door behind her.

"Rats," Fiona whispered to herself.

"Just where is New Mexico?" Simon asked. He had arrived after Fiona's desperate phone call. He didn't seem as upset as Fiona thought he should be. He pushed his glasses up on his nose and got down the atlas from the bookshelf.

"Wherever it is, I'm not going!" Fiona said. She was curled up in the armchair like a little ball, her head resting on her arms.

Simon looked up from his book and smiled. "Your parents seem to think you are," he said. He was a thin, dark boy with big brown eyes, made even larger by his heavy-rimmed glasses, and eyelashes that were far too long and far too curly for a boy. When he smiled, his whole face lit up as if someone had turned on a switch. It

8

was one of the things Fiona liked most about him.

That day, however, she did not find his smile enchanting. She peered over her arms and frowned at him. "I thought you'd be on my side," she said. "And I rather wish my parents would make me go. My mother said the final decision is up to me but that I'd regret it all my life if I didn't go. If they'd only force me, at least I could hate them for it! As it is now, the only thing I can do is hate myself. If I stay, I'll be disappointing my parents. If I go, I'll be miserable."

Simon continued to flick through the pages of the atlas. "Oh, Simon, do put that book down and think!" Fiona snapped. "There must be some way out of it. Can't you think of something? You could hide me somewhere."

Simon smiled again. "Well, I wouldn't mind hiding you over at my house, but I don't think my parents would approve."

Fiona smiled, too, uncurling like a cat, and went over to him, draping her arms around his shoulders. "Oh, Simon, what am I going to do? I really don't want to go. I feel so frightened every time I think about it. I've never been away from home before, and I don't know anything about America and—"

"Ah, here it is, New Mexico," Simon said triumphantly. "It's next to Arizona and Texas."

Fiona peered over his shoulder at the map.

"There's nothing there," she said bleakly. "Look, hardly any big towns. They want to send me to the middle of nowhere!"

Simon patted her hand. "Cheer up," he said. "Most people would envy you. I know I'd go to America like a shot if anyone offered to send me."

"Simon, you wouldn't!" Fiona gasped in horror. "You mean you wouldn't mind leaving me? Don't you care about me at all? One of the things I dread most is leaving you behind."

"It would only be about nine months, just a school year," Simon said, "not a lifetime, you know. And I really believe we should take all the opportunities we can while we are young. One day we'll be old and tied down and won't be able to travel anymore. Besides, the time is coming soon enough when we are going to go different ways. I'll be going to university in a year, don't forget."

"But that means we'll be missing our last year together," Fiona said in a sad little voice.

Simon grinned at her. "Oh, you'll forget me in a couple of weeks, I expect. You'll meet some strong ranch hand or something, and when a letter comes from me, you'll say, 'Simon who?' "

Fiona's arms tightened around Simon's shoulders. "Don't say things like that, even just to tease me. You know I could never forget you. And if I have to go, I'll write every day, I promise. And I won't even look at any ranch hands."

Simon put down the atlas and enclosed her in his arms. "I'll miss you very much," he said softly, "but I still think you'd be foolish to turn down an opportunity like this." Then he kissed her gently. When he let her go, he brushed her hair back from her face. "Those ranch hands may be better at roping steers," he said, "but I bet they're not better kissers!"

"I'll let you know when I've had a chance to compare," she said cheekily.

"I thought you just promised me you wouldn't even look at the ranch hands," Simon said, pretending to act hurt.

Fiona stroked his cheek lovingly. "You really don't have to worry, Simon," she said. Then she turned away from him to look at the map again, trying to turn contour lines into a mental picture of a landscape. High and dry, mountains and deserts, parched red earth where rain never fell came to her mind. It was so different from London that she shuddered and took Simon's hand. "Well, one thing's good, I suppose," she said shakily. "I'd be living with Professor West. I mean, I know he's a normal sort of human being, and he's a history professor, so we'll be living in a university town. It can't be that much different from life here, can it? Even if it *is* in the middle of the desert."

Chapter Two

Fiona recognized Sherry West the moment she came out of the customs area at the airport. It had seemed like an eternity of standing and waiting for Sherry's Pan Am flight to clear customs, and Fiona had worried all the while. What if they didn't recognize her and she left in a taxi and got lost in London? What if she was absolutely horrible and they didn't get along at all? Then Sherry would write home and say what a terrible person Fiona was, and when she arrived in New Mexico, everyone would hate her on sight.

Once she'd decided to go, Fiona had pushed the trip to America to the back of her mind. She knew it was something that was going to have to happen one day, like having her wisdom teeth taken out, but that day had seemed comfortably far away. But now that they were at the airport, waiting for Sherry to come through those sliding doors, the day was no longer just an unpleasant prospect for the future. It was only two weeks away. The moment Sherry stepped through the doors the countdown would begin.

Her mother didn't seem to notice how nervous Fiona was. She chatted away nonstop, as usual, interested in everything that was going on around her. "Oooh, darling, look at that beautiful dress. I bet she's just come from Paris. And that tan! Where do you think he got that tan when everyone has had such a bad summer? Goodness, look at that rude man. He almost knocked over that family with his baggage cart, and he didn't even apologize! Really, the type of people they are letting into England these days. You're not too cold, are you? This air conditioning is a little too fierce, I think. Are you sure you don't want my sweater, at least round your shoulders?"

Luckily, all Fiona was required to do was say yes, no, or really at intervals and not pay much attention. She had become very skilled at it, so she could devote all her time to serious, uninterrupted worrying.

But the moment Sherry came through the door Fiona's worries vanished. She looked exactly like her photo, so there was no chance of missing her, and she seemed so nice and friendly that Fiona knew it would be impossible not to get on with her. The one thing Fiona was not prepared for was her size. With a father who towered over most English people, she had expected a tall Sherry. The photo only showed her head and shoulders, and so it came as quite a shock to see a short, slim person waving madly at them.

"You've just got to be the Henleys," she said, without waiting for them to speak to her. "You're just like your snapshots. I'd have recognized you anywhere."

Then she smiled at them—a big, beaming smile from ear to ear—and gave Fiona's mother a hug. Fiona, who didn't come from the sort of family who hugged strangers, was rather shocked by this, but her mother looked pleased. "Well, isn't this nice," she said, beaming back at Sherry. "We've looked forward to your coming all summer, Sherry, dear."

"So have I," Sherry exclaimed. "I've been checking off the days on a big calendar on my wall, and the last few nights I could hardly sleep I was so excited. Boy, what an adventure for a girl like me! The only big city I've been to in my whole life is Los Angeles. Dad made London sound so exciting I just couldn't wait to get here!"

Fiona continued to look at Sherry in amazement. She always felt shy around new people, especially adults, and here was Sherry talking to her mother as if they were already old friends.

She looked fresh even though she'd just had a long plane trip. In fact, she sort of glowed. She stood out in the dreary London crowd. It had been a particularly wet and cold summer in London, and most people at the airport were wearing raincoats. Their skin was pale, and they all looked dull and colorless. By contrast, Sherry was wearing a pink silky jacket and pink jeans. She was even wearing pink pumps and carrying a shiny black bag over one shoulder. Her skin was beautifully tanned, and freckles were sprinkled on her nose and cheeks. Her hair would probably have been light brown if she'd spent the summer in England, but it was streaked golden by the sun.

She turned a dazzling smile on Fiona. "Well, howdy, partner!" she said. "I guess I better talk real western to you so you get used to it; otherwise, you won't understand a thing!"

Fiona smiled back. "You can't scare me like that," she said. "Don't forget we spent a year with your father, and I could understand him all right."

"Ah, but one thing he didn't tell you about himself, he's got another side to his personality. In London he may have been the serious professor, but you should see him when he's roping calves or rounding up mustangs!"

Fiona smiled again. So Sherry was going to be a tease! Well, Fiona did not intend to have her leg pulled. She grabbed one of Sherry's bags and set off for the car. "Have you traveled alone before?" she asked.

"Not far like this, but I fly to my grandmother's house in Texas and to my aunt's house in California all the time. It's cheaper than driving."

"I've never even flown before," Fiona confessed. "When we go across to France, we go by car on the Hovercraft."

"Well, I've never been to France before or on a Hovercraft, whatever that is, so that makes us even," Sherry said.

When they reached the car, Sherry picked up an enormous suitcase and swung it effortlessly into the back of the car, demonstrating to Fiona that the other girl's slender frame must be all muscle. Fiona's mother was equally impressed.

"Why, Sherry, where ever did you get so strong? I could hardly lift that case," she said.

"Oh, you build up strength roping cattle and things," Sherry said.

Fiona smiled to herself. *There she goes again,* she thought. *Trying to tease me about living in the Wild West. I bet they really live in a typical suburban house with flowerbeds in the front yard. I can't see Professor West coming within a mile of horses or cattle.*

Sherry glowed with excitement all the way home. Little things Fiona took for granted were exciting to her. "Oh, wow, look, a real double-decker bus! I've got to ride one of those things.

Oh, and look at that beautiful building. That's got to be real old."

"Only a couple hundred years," Fiona said.

Sherry giggled. "To an American a couple hundred years is very old. Albuquerque was only started in seventeen hundred, and it's one of the oldest parts of the US."

"Over here we can show you plenty of things that are a thousand years old," Fiona said. Perhaps she had sounded slightly superior, although she hadn't meant to, for Sherry answered right back.

"Of course our Indian culture goes back that far. Our New Mexico Pueblos are well over a thousand years old. Oh, look," she prattled on, "all those cute little rows of stores: Butcher Shop; Newsagent; H. Samson, Fishmonger; G. Robinson, Greengrocer," she read as they drove past. "It's just like out of an old book, and people walking around with shopping baskets, too!"

"Well, what do you do at home?" Fiona's mother sounded surprised.

"We drive to the supermarket and shop once a week," she said. "Some families shop once a month. We don't all live close to stores."

"We're getting close to home now," Fiona said. "That's the cinema I go to sometimes and the park where I play tennis."

As they turned into Fiona's street, Sherry let out a big whoop that made the other two jump.

"Holy cow!" she said. "All the way here I kept on thinking something was wrong, now I just realized what it is—you're driving on the wrong side of the street!" Sherry burst out laughing.

Sherry settled in right away. She bounced around, interested in everything, chatting to all the shopkeepers and laughing at her own mistakes. She completely charmed both Fiona's mother and father. Normally they were a quiet, serious couple, but when they talked to Sherry, they laughed. Sherry was always hugging them, and they'd hug her back. Although she knew it was mean of her, Fiona could not help feeling a stab of jealousy that Sherry had settled in so well and that everyone liked her so much. It reminded her all too painfully that her own arrival in New Mexico would probably be quite different. She'd probably be tongue-tied and shy, and her clipped English accent would come across sounding superior and rude. She wished she could be at ease with strangers the way Sherry was.

Sometimes, though, Fiona thought Sherry was a little too much at ease. She took to coming into Fiona's bedroom and curling up on the bed while Fiona did her hair or got dressed. Fiona, being an only child, was not used to near-strangers bouncing into her bedroom at all hours, but Sherry was not the sort of person you told to go away. *Heavens, I hope people*

18

don't keep walking into my room without knocking in New Mexico, she thought worriedly. *I expect there will be a lot of strange customs I shall have to get used to.*

One day Sherry came in while Fiona was folding her laundry. "I meant to ask," she said, throwing herself among the clean clothes on the bed. "You never showed me your school yet. Is it right around here?"

"Oh, no," Fiona said. "It's about half an hour away."

"I never did quite understand about the school," Sherry said. "Dad explained, but he kept saying you went to a grammar school, and that's what little kids go to over in America."

Fiona smiled. "I know, it's very confusing," she said. "Our grammar schools are just high schools that are more academic. You have to pass an exam to get in. My school is very old, with the boys' and girls' schools right next to each other."

"Oh, wow, you mean I get to ride to school on one of those big red buses?" Sherry asked, her whole face lighting up.

"Not to school you don't," Fiona said. "I walk or go by tube."

"You what?"

"I go by tube."

"You're putting me on," Sherry said suspiciously. "What sort of tube?"

Fiona looked up from her folding and saw

19

Sherry's forehead wrinkled into a worried frown. She laughed as she realized. "Oh, sorry. I didn't realize you wouldn't know what I meant. We call the underground train the tube in London."

Sherry scratched her head. "I guess I've got a lot of learning ahead of me," she said. "I thought for a moment you had some new form of transport here. You know, something out of the future where you get sucked in at one end and spat out at the other."

That was only one of the confusions they had over language. Until then Fiona had always thought that Americans spoke English. Now she knew this was not entirely true. Sherry kept running into words that meant something totally different in England.

For instance, on her first night in England Sherry offered to help Fiona's mother serve the dinner. When Mrs. Henley asked her to go to the kitchen and fetch the plate of biscuits for dessert, Sherry came back empty-handed and rather confused. "I couldn't find them," she explained, embarrassed.

Fiona ran into the kitchen and got the plate that was sitting in plain view on the counter.

"Oh, those *cookies*," Sherry laughed at herself. "In America biscuits are something different, sort of like what you call scones over here."

That was one of the nice things about Sherry. She was always ready to laugh. Even after a day, Fiona felt that Sherry could have become a best friend. It seemed a shame that they were going to be thousands of miles apart all year when they could have helped each other so much.

"I wish you were going to be there to show me around," Fiona said the second night after supper.

"Oh, you'll do just fine," Sherry said. "The kids are real friendly. They're all looking forward to meeting an English girl. You won't have any problems. Except my brother, of course. He's a big pain. But so are all brothers, aren't they?"

"I don't know, I've never had one," Fiona said. "Tell me about your family."

"There's not much to tell," Sherry said. "You'll see when you get there. There's just my brother Taco, my dad, me, and Maria Alvarez and her husband, Enrique, in the house."

"What happened to your Mum?"

"She died."

"Oh, I'm sorry."

"It's OK. I was real little when she died. I don't even remember her too well. Taco remembers her more than I do. Maria takes good care of us."

"Is she the housekeeper then?"

"I suppose so," Sherry said. "She's more like a second mother to us now. And she's a fantastic cook. You wait till you've tasted Maria's chili and tacos. That's why they call my brother Taco.

When he was little, he was just crazy about Maria's tacos; in fact, that was one of the first words he learned to say."

Fiona stared out of the window, watching raindrops trying to catch one another on the glass. The names of unfamiliar foods conjured up that strange landscape of deserts, cactuses, and cowboys. It obviously had the same effect on Sherry. She sighed. "Boy, all this talking about chili's making me feel homesick. I miss all my friends already. Right now I even miss old Richie."

"Who's that?"

"My boyfriend," Sherry said. She wrinkled her nose and made a face. "Or more like my ex-boyfriend. He was becoming a pain. I was glad to leave him behind for a while."

"What was the matter with him?" Fiona asked.

Sherry sighed. "Boring! That's what the matter was. All he can think of is tinkering with old cars and reading racing magazines and talking about racing cars he's going to build one day. No, come to think of it, I don't miss Richie at all." She laughed.

Fiona still stared out of the window. "I shall miss Simon terribly," she said.

Sherry had just met Simon. "Don't worry about him, I'll take real good care of him for you," she said with a cheeky grin. "I think he's a cutie-pie."

Fiona didn't say anything, but that night she

worried even more. She knew that Sherry had just been teasing her about Simon, but she knew that Simon was, as Sherry put it, a "cutie-pie." Would he wait a whole year for her? What would she do if she came home and found Simon going out with another girl? Fiona fell asleep to troubled dreams.

After that she hardly had time to worry. There was so much to be done. She had to go through her wardrobe, deciding what she wanted to leave behind, what she needed to buy, and what she had to wash, iron, and pack.

"Is this all right?" she kept asking Sherry. "Will I look stupid if I wear this?"

"Honey, if you just stick to shorts and jeans you can't go wrong," Sherry said kindly.

"But what about special days and dinner parties and things?"

Sherry laughed. "The only dinner parties you'll be likely to get at our house will be barbecue cookouts, and that pretty dress would likely get scorched by the fire. You can bring some nice jeans like my pink ones for parties and things. That's what most of the girls wear."

Fiona was glad she had Sherry there. It saved her from making horrible mistakes. For one thing, Fiona thought she'd need only summer clothes in New Mexico.

"But we get snow in winter!" Sherry protested.

"How can you that far south?" Fiona asked,

checking the map she'd pinned on the wall over her bed.

"We're very high up, don't forget," Sherry said. "Our house is around seven thousand feet above sea level."

Fiona found it hard enough to imagine the desert and the cactuses and blue skies. Now she tried to adjust the picture to put snow in it. "I can't believe you really have snow," she said.

"You wait until my father wakes you up at six in the morning to take feed out to the cattle because there's a foot of snow on the ground," Sherry said. "Then you'll be able to believe it all right."

"Oh, come on," Fiona said uneasily. "I do wish you wouldn't keep teasing me, I'm nervous enough as it is."

"You don't believe me about the cattle and the snow?"

"Well, I'm sure there are cattle and it does snow, but I can't imagine your father being involved. He seems much too civilized. When he was here, he just sat and read books on cold days and went to museums and things. Not the sort of man who would want to feed cattle."

Sherry shrugged her shoulders. "You'll see soon enough," she said.

Chapter Three

Fiona thought about that conversation again as the plane began its approach into Albuquerque. Before, there had been too many other things to do and think about, such as saying goodbye to her parents and Simon, trying not to cry at the airport, and trying not to show how scared she was about leaving everything safe and secure to fly halfway around the world. If her parents had been there alone, Fiona knew she probably would have allowed herself to cry. She still hadn't quite forgiven them for sending her, and it wouldn't have done any harm to make them feel a bit guilty. But Sherry had come to the airport, and so had Simon. Fiona was certainly not going to cry in front of Sherry because she didn't want her to think that English girls were cowards. And she wasn't going to cry in front of Simon because that would make her mascara run, and she didn't want his last memory of her to be with red eyes and black-streaked cheeks.

After her goodbyes she had been too worried about the actual flight to think of anything else. First she worried that the plane would crash when it took off, then that one of the wings would fall off during the flight, then that her visa and passport wouldn't be the correct ones to let her into America.

Now, as she sat back in her seat, comfortably cozy after a good lunch, she was amazed at how smoothly everything had gone. She'd even managed to cross Kennedy Airport by herself and find the connecting flight. For the first time she realized that she was actually feeling excited. *How about that,* she thought. *I've gone halfway round the world by myself. I wonder what the girls at school would think if they could see me sitting up here on a plane in the middle of America, sipping my soda like a seasoned traveler.*

She was in the middle of a pleasant daydream, in which she was showing pictures of New Mexico to all the kids at school while they clustered round admiringly, when an announcement made her sit up with a start.

"Ladies and gentlemen, we shall be landing at Albuquerque Sunport shortly. Please fasten your seat belts and extinguish all cigarettes."

Fiona fished around but couldn't find half of

26

her seat belt. She blew her whole image of the cool world traveler by having to get the flight attendant to lean over and buckle it up for her. She peered out of the window. The plane was definitely coming down now. When she had looked out before, all she'd seen were clouds or tiny squares of fields. Now she could see reddish-brown mountains clearly and dry, brown valleys and patches of green around towns and lakes. Then she could make out roads and trails, then little antlike specks on the roads that turned into cars. New Mexico was actually below her; Professor West would be waiting for her. . . .

How would she survive a whole year in this strange, sunburned place? Would it really be like the Wild West, or had Sherry just been teasing her? Would the kids accept a complete stranger? What if no one talked to her for a whole year? What if she met a rattlesnake?

Will you relax, she told herself firmly. *You are getting quite upset over nothing. There isn't a thing to worry about. After all, you know Professor West; you know that he isn't a wild cowboy. He surely lives a perfectly ordinary life in a nice, ordinary house.* She closed her eyes and tried to picture the house, a sort of western version of her house in London: its walls lined with books and Professor West sitting quietly reading and smoking his pipe while

27

outside strange, mad people galloped around on horses, shooting rattlesnakes with guns.

The plane was so low now that Fiona could see houses gleaming white with red-tiled roofs. Lots of them had swimming pools that looked wonderfully blue from the plane. They passed over a wide river. Now there were trees and green fields beneath them.

So much for the desert, she thought, surprised. *It's not so different from England after all. I've been worrying for nothing.* Then the plane touched down and roared to a halt.

As she stepped out of the plane, the first thing that struck Fiona was the dry heat. It was like opening an oven door. The next was the light. It was so much brighter than in London. She had to screw up her eyes against the sunshine. The air was so incredibly clear that everything seemed to glow—the red of the mountains, the brilliant blue sky, the gleaming white buildings. Everything was bigger and brighter, stranger and more overpowering than Fiona had ever imagined. What she would have liked to do was turn right around and go home. Instead, she walked forward slowly and hesitantly, as if she were stepping into a dream world in which Professor West was the only safe, real point.

Suddenly she spotted his face in the crowd. He was waiting behind the barrier for her. But he was strangely transformed. In London he had worn a dark business suit, like her father, or a sweater and cords on weekends, but the man walking toward her and smiling was not the same. He *belonged* in this frightening dream world. He was wearing faded blue jeans and an open-necked check shirt. Worse still, he was wearing cowboy boots with tall heels and a real cowboy hat on his head, so that he seemed enormous, like a strange giant who had taken over Professor West's face. By his side was a boy, almost as tall as he was and also wearing a cowboy hat. The boy was similar enough to Sherry for Fiona to guess that this was Taco. He had the same freckles over a deep golden tan, the same sun-streaked hair poking out from beneath his hat, and his eyes were an alarming bright blue, almost as blue as the New Mexico sky. Although he was slim, he was by no means skinny, and his suntanned arms looked really muscular. He came toward Fiona now, but his greeting was quite different from Sherry's. He stared at her with an appraising, almost hostile scowl.

"Well, here she is," Professor West said warmly in his deep rumbling voice, "and right on time, too." He stretched out his hand to her, grasping it in a firm handshake. "Let's go down and find your luggage. How was your flight?" he asked.

"Very nice, thank you," Fiona mumbled.

Professor West laughed. "That's the English for you, Taco," he said. "They'd say 'Very nice, thank you,' even if they were scared silly or one wing had fallen off the plane! Taco, this is Fiona Henley," Professor West went on as warmly as ever. "Fiona, this is my son, Taco."

"Hi," Taco mumbled. "You want me to go and get the truck while you pick up the bags, Dad?" Without waiting for an answer, he turned his back on them and disappeared into the crowd.

"Don't mind Taco," Professor West said to Fiona as they made their way through the airport crowd to the baggage area. "It takes him awhile with new people. We lead a kind of cutoff life, and he's always been a bit shy around strangers. He'll be fine when he gets used to you."

Fiona nodded, but she couldn't think of anything else to say. Her legs were feeling shaky, partly from sitting still on the long flight, partly because she was scared and Taco's scowl had hardly made her feel any better. *I'm shy, too,* she thought, *but I'm not rude like that. It can't just be shyness. He doesn't want me here.* Fiona waited quietly next to Professor West until her three brown cases finally appeared. She listened to the people talking all around her in the American accents that sounded so strange. It was the way people spoke in movies.

"Come on," Professor West said, leading her out through the glass doors into the dazzling sunlight. "Where's that boy gone?" he asked, looking around. "He said he was fetching the

30

truck for us—oh, there he is, way down there!" He waved violently. A red pickup roared to life and came screeching to a halt beside them. Professor West opened the cab door for Fiona and helped her climb up. It was hard in the tight skirt she was wearing. She sat down next to Taco. The boy continued to stare straight ahead as if she didn't exist.

Wanting to break the uneasy silence, she made up her mind to be brave and speak first. "It must be hard to drive a big truck like this," she said hesitantly. "Have you been driving long?"

Taco pushed his hat back on his head. "I've been driving trucks since I was ten years old," he said.

"Heavens," Fiona said, impressed. "What age are you allowed to drive here then?"

"Sixteen officially," he answered, "but nobody cares on the ranch."

"Well, I'm sixteen, but I don't think I could handle driving a truck yet," she said.

He shot her a brief look that said clearly, "Of course a weak little English girl like you couldn't drive a truck!" Then he continued to stare straight ahead of him in silence.

After loading Fiona's cases, Professor West swung himself into the cab, and Taco drove off. Fiona watched the clean, modern high-rise offices of Albuquerque roll by. They passed the University of New Mexico where Professor West taught, and Fiona was surprised when he told her that the strange modernistic style of the buildings was copied from the old Indian pueblos. They drove through Old Town, and Fiona liked the look of the plaza with its big shady trees and old Spanish houses. She was pleased to see art galleries and boutiques. *Not primitive at all,* she thought.

Then the truck swung through expensive suburbs where more Spanish-style houses were surrounded by green lawns, each with sprinklers going furiously.

"There's so little rain here that you have to water a lawn almost constantly to keep it green," Professor West explained.

"I expect Sherry told you quite a bit about our place," Professor West said.

"No, not much," Fiona said. "She kept telling me I'd see for myself."

"Well, it's nothing fancy," Professor West said. "And of course, we're quite a ways out of town, but we're kind of proud of it. My grandpa homesteaded it and tried to grow crops there, but of course he soon found out it wasn't much use for anything but cattle." They were going faster now, the only vehicle on the open road. There were fields beside them and patches of woodland, contrasting with the stark, bony bareness of the mountains beyond. "The land down here is irrigated by the Rio Grande," Professor West said. "That's how it stays so nice and green.

We're farther away, and water is a big headache for us."

Fiona could see that for herself as they turned off the highway. Away from the green valley, the fields turned into scrub with low bushes and yellow earth showing through sparse grass. Gone were the orderly buildings of the city, the green lawns and neat front yards. Fiona felt a horrible sinking feeling in her stomach. Everything Sherry had said was true. She hadn't been teasing at all about roping calves and feeding cattle in the snow. *I want to go home*, rose up in Fiona's throat. She almost said it out loud just as Taco turned the truck onto a bumpy road and under a wooden gate with the sign BAR W RANCH over it.

"Well, here we are," Professor West said cheerfully. "This is home. What do you think of it?"

"It's lovely," Fiona managed to say with her typical English politeness.

Chapter Four

The truck came to a halt outside a low, white-washed house. A wooden veranda ran the whole length of it, making a deep pool of shade. The roofs of both were red tile. It was late afternoon, and the house and the large tree growing beside it threw a fierce black shadow across the dusty yard. Around the house grew some tired, dusty-looking oleanders. There was a small garden to the right with tall cornstalks peeping over a dangerous-looking cactus hedge. There was a barn, and beyond that was scrub, no fences, no fields, just gently rising scrubland that blended into the haze at the base of the mountains. It might have been the middle of nowhere.

"It gets real pretty around sunset," Professor West said. "Come on in, and I'll show you your room." They walked up onto the tile-roofed porch, then in through the heavy doorway. The house walls seemed to be about a yard thick. Professor West slapped one. "Adobe," he said.

"I beg your pardon?" Fiona said.

"Adobe, that's what these walls are made of. You just cut blocks from the adobe clay soil, mix in some sand, and let it harden in the sun. Then you cover it with lime, and you've got yourself a house that stays cool in summer and warm in winter. My grandfather built this with his own hands."

Fiona had to agree the house was delightfully cool. It was like stepping into a cold shower after the heat outside. She followed the professor along a dark hallway until he opened a door at the end. It was a nice room, large and simply furnished with a big, old-fashioned bed and chest. Fiona wished that Sherry had been there, too. It would have been more bearable if she'd been beside her, laughing and cheering her up when she needed it—and she needed it right then.

"I'll be right back," Professor West said. "Make yourself comfortable." Fiona nodded.

It was a shock being in a strange room and realizing that it was going to be *her* room for a whole year, that for the first time her parents were not within calling distance and that the only people close by were a man who spent most of his time buried in books and a boy who clearly didn't want her around. All that, plus the tiredness of a long plane ride and jet lag, brought Fiona very close to tears. How was she ever going to make any friends stuck way out here? How was she even going to get to school? How was she going to survive a whole year? Fiona brushed back the tears that were starting to sting. She looked down at her watch. Five o'clock, New Mexico time. If it were five o'clock in England, her mother would be clearing away the tea table, chattering all the time to her father, who would answer only in grunts. And Simon would be dropping by to do some homework or to play the guitar with her. But it wasn't five o'clock in England. It was already the middle of the night. For the first time it really sank in that she was half a world away from home.

Oh well, I suppose I had better go out and see if I can help with my bags, she thought. She opened her door and found herself face to face with a strange man. Old nightmares about bandits and gunslingers came rushing in on her. She let out a short, sharp shriek as she slammed the door. Her scream brought Professor West and Taco rushing in from outside.

"What's wrong, Fiona?" Professor West yelled through the door.

"I opened the door, and I saw this face outside," she said peering into the hall.

Professor West laughed kindly. "This is Enrique. He's bringing in your bags for you."

Enrique grinned sheepishly. "I was just putting down the bags to knock on her door when she opened it," he said. "I sure didn't mean to scare her. To tell the truth, she scared me, too, when she screamed like that!"

"Anyone would be scared to see your ugly face for the first time," Taco said teasingly.

Enrique laughed loudly. "I'm sorry I scared you, miss. I'll bring the bags in now." And he pushed past her into the room.

"Are you all right now, Fiona?" Professor West asked.

She nodded. "I'm sorry to make such a fuss. It's just that I wasn't expecting anyone—"

"That's quite understandable," Professor West interrupted.

"Maybe you should take her down to the kitchen and introduce her to Maria before she screams at her, too," Taco said dryly, and Fiona knew he thought she made a stupid fuss over nothing.

As it was, she realized that she might well have screamed at the sight of Maria if she'd met her for the first time in a dark passage. Maria was huge, almost as wide as she was high. She was standing next to a big black iron stove in a large, dark kitchen, but her presence seemed to fill the whole room. She was wearing a red-flowered skirt and a bright yellow blouse. Her black hair was piled up and anchored with silver combs. The colors would have looked gaudy on anyone else, but on Maria they looked just right. She had at least three chins, and her face was creased into a hundred laugh lines.

"So, here she is," Maria said, waddling toward Fiona, Taco, and Professor West. "She got here at last. Poor little thing, she looks so pale and thin. She needs fattening up a bit with my good cooking! Come over here, little one." She took Fiona's hand and led her to the table. "Sit yourself down. You must be tired, such a long trip in a plane! I went on a plane once from here to Los Angeles for my sister's wedding. After that trip I was tired. They don't make airplane seats for people my size."

"I heard about that flight," Taco said. "They had a real weight problem, and the plane had to fly all the way to Los Angeles with one wing down!"

Maria laughed until her body shook like Jell-O. "You terrible boy, why do you always say such bad things? Don't you believe one word he tells you, miss. How do you say your name again?"

"Fiona."

"Fiona," she tried out the word, rolling it around her tongue. "Fiona. That's a pretty name. Is it Italian?"

Fiona laughed. "No, it's Scottish. My mother's family came from Scotland."

"Well, it's a real pretty name for a real pretty girl. I hope you're going to feel right at home here," Maria said.

"Thank you," Fiona answered. "I hope I shall, too."

"Ay, ay, ay!" Maria suddenly exploded. "Look at the time. Now will all of you get out of my kitchen so that we can eat before midnight."

Fiona was glad to go. This giant of a woman who talked in a little gentle voice one minute and roared like a lion the next was a little hard to take when she was so tired.

"OK, we get the hint," Taco said. "I hope you remember what I told you about the special meal tonight."

"I remember," Maria roared. "What do you think I am—stupid?"

"She's a bit emotional," Professor West told Fiona as he led her into the high-ceilinged living room, "but she's a real honey. She's married to Enrique, by the way. He helps out on the ranch, and she takes care of the house. They've been with us since before the kids were born. Maria helped raise Taco and Sherry after their mother died. They both adore her."

"Are you going to help me get that hay out before dinner, Dad?" Taco called down the hallway.

Professor West turned toward the door. "Oh, yes, we'd better do that tonight. Excuse us awhile, Fiona. Make yourself at home. There's soda in the refrigerator if you want some."

Fiona sat in a big leather armchair and looked out the window. The truck was bumping across the scrub with a load of hay bales on the back. The setting sun hung like a red ball above the purple hills, painting the high mountains to the east with fire. The room was cool and dark. In one corner was an open brick fireplace. Beautifully woven Indian rugs were hung on the walls and lay on the floor. A wooden case displayed all sorts of Indian pottery. There were no books on the walls as Fiona had expected. From far away came the mooing of cows and the harsh screech of an unknown bird. Fiona felt totally alone.

I wanted to make a good impression to start with, she thought, *but already they think of me as a weirdo, someone who screams at the drop of a hat. I won't ever fit in here.* She looked longingly at the telephone. How nice it would be to pick it up and hear her mother's voice on the other end. *But then it would only be worse than ever when I had to put the phone down and know she was so far away,* she thought.

Professor West and Taco didn't reappear until it was quite dark. Night came on suddenly there, which was a shock for Fiona. In England the summer evenings were light and long, with the day gradually fading around eight or nine. Here, the sun set around seven. One minute it was there, resting on the horizon, then it was gone. The sky glowed for a few seconds, then the world was plunged into total darkness. *Even a foreign sunset,* Fiona thought.

Dinner was served in the tiled kitchen, which looked much friendlier now that the lights were on. Taco had changed out of his jeans with the torn knee, putting on a newer pair with a black T-shirt with "Truth or Consequences" on the front of it and "District Rodeo Champ" on the back in silver letters. In the warm glow of the light, his skin looked a rich golden color and his eyes incredibly bright. Fiona couldn't help noticing how handsome he was. His eyes seemed to be laughing as he watched her come into the room, as if he were enjoying a secret joke. She felt herself blush when his gaze met hers.

At least that's better than the scowl, Fiona thought.

When they were all seated, Maria came waddling over to the table carrying a steaming bowl. "Here you are, Fionacita, I made your favorite," she said putting it down in front of Fiona. "Taco tells me you like your chili extra spicy hot, so I make it like that, just for you."

Fiona looked up to meet Taco's amused smile. His face was a picture of perfect innocence. *No wonder he was laughing,* Fiona thought angrily. *He'd been planning a perfectly horrible trick.*

"Taco," Professor West said testily, "you know Fiona has never tried chili before. Maria's will burn her mouth off. That was a stupid, childish joke!"

Fiona felt her face going red as anger boiled up inside her. Taco West was not going to get the better of her that easily! "That's quite all right, Professor West," she said sweetly. "You see, back in England I eat Indian and Pakistani food all the time, and that's quite as spicy as this, I'm sure. I know I'm going to enjoy it." She leaned forward and took a generous helping of the chili. She took a bite. It really did burn her mouth and throat, but she was determined to finish it all without taking a sip of water.

"That was great," she said once her bowl was empty. She turned to Taco and gave him a triumphant smile.

That night as she climbed into bed, her mouth and throat still smarting from the chili, she suddenly felt much better and more hopeful. "No more feeling sorry for myself," she said, staring up at the rough plaster ceiling. "So Taco thinks I'm a weak and feeble little English girl and that he's going to get a good laugh out of me. Well, let him try. I'll show him I'm not nearly so weak and feeble as he thinks!"

But the next morning Fiona found that getting the better of Taco was not going to be that easy. She woke up early, unaccustomed to the quiet. In London the outside noises never ceased: buses, airplanes, newsboys, even sparrows and starlings. But here, Fiona could almost feel the silence. She opened her eyes, gradually focusing on the unfamiliar room and the strange lack of noise. It was so quiet that she found herself holding her breath, waiting for something to happen.

She climbed out of bed and walked to the window. The slate-tiled floor felt cold to her feet. Outside the sun had not yet risen, but the sky in the east glowed as if it were about to burst into flame. The earth was totally still. Nothing moved as far as Fiona could see, not even a breath of wind through the gray scrub. Then, suddenly, a cock crowed, making Fiona jump. As if the crow were a signal, the world seemed to come awake. The sun flamed over the horizon, chickens started clucking, and the dull thud of hoofbeats could be heard going away over the soft ground.

Fiona showered in her own bathroom, a real luxury in England, and put on blue jeans and a bright green sweatshirt. She noticed how pale her skin looked against the green. *I really must do something about getting a tan fast,* she thought. *Otherwise, I shall look like a freak among all these tanned people.* Then she brushed out her hair, wishing she hadn't been so lazy the night before about getting out all the tangles. At last she was satisfied with the result and tied her blond hair to one side with a green ribbon.

She went down to the kitchen and found Maria already busy. That day she was wearing an orange- and pink-striped housecoat that made her look like a hot-air balloon. She beamed when she saw Fiona. "Ah, buenos días, good morning, you're just in time. Pour yourself some coffee and sit down," she called. "I'm just fixing breakfast."

Fiona helped herself to coffee, not daring to mention that she always had tea at home and didn't like coffee very much. The coffee tasted strong but good, and Fiona realized that she was positively starved. *If Mum could see me now*, she thought. At home she always had to be dragged out of bed just in time to rush to school. She never managed to eat more than half a piece of toast. That day she felt as if she could eat a horse—until she saw what was put before her. It was a huge stack of pancakes, surrounded by strips of bacon. Fiona eyed them suspiciously. At home she ate pancakes rarely, usually on Pancake Day—the English Mardi Gras, which the not-so-excitable British celebrated only by making pancakes. Fiona's family occasionally served pancakes as dessert, with lemon and sugar. She had never thought of having them for breakfast and certainly never with bacon. What were you meant to do, eat the bacon first and leave the pancakes until later? She was too shy to ask, but the question was answered for her by Maria, who picked up a jug and poured a cascade of sticky brown syrup over the whole plate for her. "Here, you need a good helping of syrup," she said.

Fiona watched in horror as the brown river flowed slowly down the stack of pancakes and over the bacon. She tried to pull a strip of bacon clear, but the sweet puddle just kept spreading. In the end she gave up and ate pancakes, bacon, and syrup. The final flavor was not bad at all.

She had almost finished when Taco walked in. He was wearing dirty old jeans and smelled strongly of horse. "Where's my breakfast, Maria, I'm dying of hunger," he called as he helped himself to coffee.

Maria eyed him critically. "You'd better go and wash those dirty hands and face before you get anything to eat here," she said. "You've been out riding already?"

"Sure. I took Red Fox out again."

"How's he coming along?"

"Still fights like a devil, but I'm going to get him licked one of these days. At least he doesn't buck me off *all* the time now."

"Does your father know you took Red Fox?"

"Ah, Maria, he's not even awake yet."

Maria flipped a pancake skillfully. "But I remember quite clearly when he told you he didn't want you breaking any horses alone." She put a pancake on top of the ever-growing stack. "And especially not Red Fox."

Taco went over to the sink and splashed wa-

45

ter over his face and hands. "I can handle him," he said scornfully. "He acts mean, but he's a pussycat."

"You wait until you're lying out there in the middle of nowhere with a broken leg," Maria said. "Then maybe you'll remember what your papa tells you about going off alone on unbroken horses."

Taco went around the table toward Maria and draped his arms round her neck. "Yeah, but you're not going to say anything, are you, dear, sweet, kind Maria?"

Maria shook him off. "Oh, go away. You're always doing far too much sweet talking." She looked across to Fiona. "Don't you believe a thing this boy tells you, you hear? He would talk the hind legs off a donkey."

Until that moment Fiona had felt totally invisible and rather uncomfortable, listening in on someone else's argument. Now Taco seemed to notice her for the first time. His eyes looked at her critically, then seemed to approve of what he saw. "Oh, hi," he said, then ignored her again as he attacked a giant stack of pancakes.

How hard it is to understand people, Fiona thought as she watched Taco eating. *He has made it quite clear that he doesn't like me, so why did he look at me that way?*

Professor West came in shortly afterward, looking more as Fiona remembered him in London, dressed in dark pants and a crisp white shirt.

46

"Hi, everyone," he said. "No breakfast for me, Maria. I have to run. I have a faculty meeting at eight-thirty sharp. Can you imagine that, actually hoping to get an entire faculty together at eight-thirty in the morning when they've had the whole summer off? It will take a miracle."

"Can I ride into town with you?" Taco asked. "I need to do a lot of things before school starts next week."

"Actually, I hoped you'd stick around and keep Fiona company," his father said.

Taco gave Fiona a quick glance. "She can come, too," he said quickly. "I can drive her around in the truck while you have your meeting and show her beautiful downtown Albuquerque."

Professor West seemed to consider this. At last he shook his head. "No, not today, son. I might be in the meeting all day, and I don't want Fiona to have to hang around that long in the sun. Remember, she's not used to this heat yet. Give her awhile to settle in and take things gently."

"Oh, but don't let me stop you going," Fiona said hastily. "I shall be quite all right here."

"Nonsense. Taco would love to stay and keep you company, wouldn't you, Taco?" his father said firmly.

"Sure, Dad," Taco mumbled. He got up to go out.

"Hey, Taco," his father called to him. "Why

don't you take Fiona out in the *bosque* before it gets too hot?"

Taco looked at her. "You want to ride in the bosque?" he asked.

Fiona felt confused. She guessed a bosque must be some sort of carriage. "I never went in one," she said. "What is it?"

Taco laughed. Professor West smiled, too. "Bosque," Taco said. "That means the woods in Spanish, all those cottonwood trees down by the stream. We call that bosque. It's nice to ride there before the sun gets too hot. Oh, but you probably don't know how to ride a horse, do you?"

Now it was not strictly true that Fiona had never ridden a horse before. She had ridden ponies on the beach a couple of times, holding onto the saddle desperately whenever the pony trotted. At one stage she had decided she wanted to take riding lessons, and she'd gone to a riding school on Hampstead Heath. It had been a rainy day, and she'd fallen off in the middle of the mud, which had made her decide she didn't want to ride after all. But something about Taco's laughter and his tone of voice made her feel brave. "Of course I can ride," she heard herself saying and immediately wished she hadn't.

"Great," Taco said. "I'll go saddle up a couple of horses. I'd go put on some old jeans if I were you. Those look much too good to ride in."

Well, Fiona thought as she changed her

48

clothes, *at least he liked my outfit*. Then she began to realize what she had committed herself to. She stood there, hesitating between going out, canceling the ride, and looking like a fool, or going ahead, falling off, and looking like a fool, anyway. *Of course, I am meant to be taking it easy today, Professor West's orders*, she reassured herself. *If we start to do anything I can't handle, which will probably be anything more than a walk, I'll just tell Taco I feel too tired.*

But still she found her knees shaking as she thought about riding beside a boy who was a rodeo champion. She had to try, she decided. She was going to have to ride one day, so she might as well start then. Besides, she didn't want Taco to think she was a coward. But why should it matter what he thought? she wondered. She couldn't really find him attractive, could she?

Fiona's emotions confused her. *Of course he's attractive, but that doesn't mean I like him. I just don't want him to get the better of me, that's all.*

As she finished tying her sneakers, she heard Taco and his father pass by outside her window.

"Which horses are you taking?" his father asked.

"I thought I'd give her Princess," Taco's voice came back. "She needs the exercise."

"Princess, are you crazy?"

"Well, she said she could ride, didn't she?"

"Yes, but not Princess. You know all her funny habits. She's not an easy horse, not even for Sherry. Go saddle up Traveler. He's nice and gentle for a newcomer."

"Oh, but, Dad, Traveler's so slow."

"This isn't a race, Taco, and I don't want Fiona scared. Go saddle Traveler, do you hear me?"

"Sure, Dad," Taco said, sighing.

Fiona sighed, too, but with relief. She was glad that Taco and his father had had that conversation and that she'd escaped having to ride Princess. Princess sounded like a nice mild name for a horse, but Professor West hadn't made her sound mild at all. She was even hard for Sherry to ride. Thank heavens she was going to get good old Traveler, who was too slow! She felt much better as she snapped a barrette in place and went out to join Taco.

Taco helped Fiona climb into the big western saddle. He held one of her hands to steady her, and Fiona felt a gentle shiver run down her spine. Taco looked tenderly into her eyes, then brushed the moment away with a tiny scowl. He hopped nimbly onto the other horse. "Ready to go?" he asked, giving his horse a slap.

They left the dusty ranch and headed down a trail. Soon they were riding between small trees and bushes. Taco went ahead. There was no sound except for the swish of the horses' legs

50

through the dry grass and the sigh of the wind in the cottonwood trees. Above their heads a large hawk drifted lazily across a rich sky. Although it was early, the sun was already hot. Fiona felt herself soaking up the quiet, breezy sunshine.

Taco turned back to her. "You OK?" he called.

Fiona nodded.

"You want to lope?"

For a second Fiona thought he'd asked if she wanted to elope with him, but then she guessed it must be another word, like bosque, that she didn't yet understand. Still, she wasn't going to admit her ignorance again. "All right," she called and waited to see what would happen next.

She regretted her answer almost immediately. Taco spurred his horse, and it sprang forward. Fiona's horse followed suit, and she had to grab onto the saddle horn to stop herself from being flung off. She remembered the time she'd fallen off the horse in England. But that time there had been nothing to hold onto, no high saddle to keep her in place. She thought that Taco would think she was a baby for clinging onto the horn so fiercely, but he was ahead of her and couldn't see. As soon as she got over her initial fright, she began to enjoy this new sensation. Loping was like a fast, easy run, and the wind in her face gave her an exciting feeling of speed.

Then the trees thinned out, and they came to

a wide meadow with the briefest glimpse of water ahead of them. Without warning, Fiona's horse threw up its head and streaked past Taco's in a flat gallop. Fiona, clinging desperately to the saddle horn, tried to pull on the reins and make it stop. Trees brushed past her, the ground flying by on either side. Then a stream was ahead of them, gleaming in the bright sun. Fiona tried to scream, but no sound would come out. The horse was heading straight for the water. It plunged down the steep bank without slowing at all. A wet spray came up all around, and still it didn't stop. Then, right in the middle of the stream, it came to a halt so suddenly that Fiona was nearly flung over its head. It lowered its head to the water and drank deeply.

The water was not deep, only up to the horse's knees, but it was swift flowing. Fiona's heart was still beating wildly from the fright. She looked around, wondering what to do next, waiting for Taco to come and rescue her. She saw him looking down from the top of the bank, a broad grin on his face. "I thought you said you could ride," he called. "Why didn't you pull her up?"

Fiona glared at him. "I might have broken my neck," she yelled, "and you would have had to explain that to your father."

"It's not my fault you can't control an easy horse," he said, pushing his hat back on his head and sitting comfortably in his saddle. "You shouldn't let her get away with it. Just pull her up and bring her out."

Fiona tried tugging on the reins to bring up the horse's head. The horse refused to move. She tried hefty kicks to the horse's side, but they had no effect, either. She was very conscious of Taco sitting there grinning. "You might come and help," she called, glaring at him.

Just then Fiona heard the clink of harnesses and the thud of hoofbeats on the opposite bank. Three riders came into view, moving fast along the water. Fiona was only too aware of how dumb she looked, sitting in the middle of a stream on a horse that wouldn't move.

Perhaps they'll think I'm letting my horse take a drink, she said to herself. *Perhaps they won't even notice me.*

But the three riders brought their mounts to a stop and looked down at her with interest. Fiona tried to pretend that they didn't exist, but she couldn't help noticing that one of them was a gorgeous girl with long, thick, wavy golden hair. Beside her were a dark-haired girl and a lanky boy. She also couldn't help noticing that all three were grinning.

"Hey, Taco, don't tell me that Princess is up to her old tricks again," the boy called.

"What are you giving this poor girl, riding lessons or swimming lessons?" the golden-haired girl asked.

"Looks like a bit of both," Taco called back.

"This must be the English girl. Some first riding lesson," the girl said, snickering.

Fiona began to feel more and more like some captive zoo animal. She felt like yelling, "Don't all just stand there and talk about me, get me out of here," but she felt close to tears and therefore not sure of her voice.

"Who else would it be, Honey?" Taco called back.

"Boy, Taco, you sure are a jerk, making her ride Princess," the black-haired, Spanish-looking girl shouted. "You know she always does this, even with Sherry. Go and get her out this minute!"

"I was just about to, Rosie, dearest," Taco said sweetly, urging his horse down the bank to Fiona. "You guys going to Wilt's tonight?"

"I'm going. So's Rosie," the boy called.

Taco started to lead Fiona's horse out of the river. It followed him meekly.

"Are you coming tonight, Honey?" he asked again.

"Only if your dad lets you have the truck," she said evenly and tossed back her gorgeous golden hair.

"Now, behave yourself, Taco, you hear?" Rosie shouted after him. "Don't you go playing any more tricks on that poor girl. And why don't you bring her over to Wilt's tonight so she can meet everyone properly?"

"Come on, Rosie, let's get moving," Honey

said. She urged on her horse. "See you tonight, Taco," she called as they galloped off.

Fiona allowed herself to be led up the bank. Anger was boiling up inside her. So this horse wasn't slow old Traveler, after all. It was Princess, who even Sherry couldn't handle! Princess with all the bad habits, like bolting into the middle of streams and rivers. *He did it quite deliberately to make a fool of me*, she thought. *And he succeeded, too. I have never felt more foolish in my whole life!*

She rode in silence, seething with anger, all the way home. Every time she sneaked a look at Taco, who still looked very pleased with himself, she felt more and more like slapping his face. They rode back up to the corral. Taco swung himself from the saddle and came around to help her dismount. This fake act of courtesy was the final straw for Fiona.

"I must say, you have some nerve," she said as he lowered her to the ground. "You put me on a horse you knew was too difficult for me to handle, just so you could get a good laugh at me. I think that's just horrible! You didn't care that I might have fallen off or hit a tree and got myself killed, did you? Well, you've made your point. You don't want me here for some reason. Just let me tell you a thing or two. I didn't want to come here, either. A primitive, uncivilized place like this was the last place on earth I wanted to be. I've had to leave behind a nice family and nice friends, all of whom know how to behave properly, and I'm stuck with a country bumpkin like you who gets his kicks out of watching horses bolt! Is this how you make someone welcome? If I'd treated your sister this badly, she would have packed her bags and flown home by now." The words all came out in a rush. When Fiona finally stopped for breath, she noticed that Taco was still holding her. "And will you get your hands off me!" she shouted. "I've had quite enough of your company for one day.".

"You know," Taco said, smiling down at her, "you're awful cute when you get mad." And before Fiona could do anything, he was pulling her toward him and kissing her full and hard on the lips.

At first she was too amazed to do anything, then she fought to get away from him. "I simply cannot believe you," she said shakily when he finally released her. "I suppose you think that standing there with your tan and your blue eyes and your muscles you are irresistible to girls. Well, I've got news for you. You might be Mr. Hot Shot out here, where there aren't many boys to choose from, but I wouldn't touch you with a ten-foot pole if you were the last boy on earth!" Then she stalked away toward the house, past a grinning Enrique, who had obviously seen and heard the whole thing.

Chapter Five

Fiona managed to avoid Taco for the rest of the day. Back in her room she became overwhelmed by tension, anger, and homesickness and cried. *I just don't understand him at all,* she thought miserably. *Why did he go and kiss me like that! I suppose he just wanted to prove that he was Mr. Macho and I was little Miss Cute and Helpless. Well, he won't come near me again after what I said to him! I'll never forgive him for that, never!* Now her eyes looked red and puffy, and she was afraid to come out and have Taco laugh at her again. But when Maria called her to lunch, she learned that Taco had gone off with Enrique, and she was able to eat her salad alone.

It was late afternoon when he came back. Fiona was sitting alone in the big, cool living room. She had written her first letter to her parents, describing the flight, the house, and the countryside and leaving out any mention of unbearable New Mexico boys. Then, with nothing else to do, she had discovered a guitar in a corner and started to strum quietly to herself. She looked up as she heard feet on the tiled floor and quickly stopped playing.

"You play pretty well," Taco said.

"Thank you," she said tonelessly and put down the guitar.

"Look," he said, "I'm sorry about this morning. It was dumb of me. Let's forget about it, can we?"

"All right," said Fiona, still not looking up.

Taco shifted his feet nervously. "So, um, do you want to come with me this evening? Some of the kids are having a barbecue."

"I don't think you really want me there," Fiona said calmly.

"Rosie wants me to bring you," he said. "She wants you to get a chance to meet all the kids before school starts."

"Oh, wonderful. I suppose they all want to have a good laugh about the horse and me," Fiona said.

"No way," Taco said. "Rosie made me promise I'd bring you. And, anyway, you can mail that letter on the way into town."

"Are you sure this isn't another joke you've cooked up?" Fiona asked, looking up coolly to meet his eyes. "Because I have no great wish to be dumped over a precipice or abandoned in the desert or anything else that might amuse you."

"I said I was sorry," Taco growled. "We'll leave about six, OK?"

"OK." Fiona managed a faint smile. "What should I wear?"

Taco shrugged his shoulders. "Any old thing will do. You look fine with what you've got on right now."

Their eyes met for a moment, each with unspoken remembrance of that kiss, then Fiona got up. "I'll be ready at six," she said coldly.

Professor West arrived home with the truck before Taco and Fiona were due to leave. If he had heard anything about the morning's episode, he wasn't letting on. He chatted pleasantly to Fiona and wished her a good evening.

Feeling more than a little scared, Fiona climbed up into the cab beside Taco. Even at home, among her friends, she wasn't very good at parties. Large numbers of people made her feel shy and tongue-tied, and she hated meeting strangers. In fact, what she liked most was to stay home with Simon and spend a quiet evening in front of the telly. Her mother, who liked talking to everyone, used to say she was a little old woman.

So what am I doing now, going to a party full of strangers I don't want to meet, with a boy who doesn't like me? she wondered. *Well, I suppose I've got to meet them sometime. I can't go through a whole year speaking to no one but Taco. And I certainly don't want to talk to him too much.*

Not that Taco was overtalkative. They sat together in silence as he drove the truck skillfully over the bumpy road. A mile or so toward town, he swung into a driveway and honked the horn loudly. A few seconds later the front door opened, and a girl came out. It was the same beautiful girl from that morning, only that night she wasn't dressed in jeans and a shirt. She was wearing a flimsy white dress with a flowing skirt and an off-the-shoulder neckline. The white fabric against her golden tan looked dramatic, and her golden hair was now falling in curls over her shoulders and down her back.

And Taco told me to wear any old thing, Fiona thought. She was sure this was another of his tricks and that when they got to the party, she would be the only girl in jeans among hundreds of girls in pretty dresses.

"Climb on up," Taco called down to the girl.

She came around and opened the passenger door. She didn't look at all pleased to see Fiona. "Oh, hi," she said flatly. She climbed up into the cab. "You're our English visitor. We didn't really get introduced this morning." Fiona smiled politely. "Well, isn't this cozy?" Honey drawled. "A real snug little threesome." She turned to

Fiona. "I guess I should introduce myself since Taco's obviously not going to. I'm Honey Lampert. I'm sure Taco's already told you *all* about me." Then she flashed Fiona a big smile that looked about as friendly as that of a hunting lioness.

"How do you do. I'm Fiona Henley," Fiona said primly.

"Well," Taco said from the driver's seat, "now we're all real friendly." He had the merest hint of a grin on his face, as if he were enjoying making Honey jealous.

"Seeing as how Fiona only just got here, we just have to find someone to give her a ride home," Honey said. "She'll be too tired to stay out real late tonight, won't she?"

It was such an obvious hint that Fiona had to smile. Honey was making it quite clear that she wanted Taco all to herself. *Well, she is welcome to him,* Fiona thought.

"I promised my dad I'd look after her tonight," Taco said, "so you might have to find someone to give you a ride home if you want to stay late."

"That won't be too hard," Honey said, cooing. "I could name half a dozen guys who would be only too willing to drive me anywhere."

"Look, I don't want to be in the way," Fiona interrupted before the argument turned into an out-and-out fight.

"Oh, don't worry, sweetie, you won't be," Honey said. "We'll fix you up with a nice guy of your own."

"I don't need fixing up with anyone," Fiona said frostily. "I have a very nice boyfriend of my own at home."

"Well, hold your hair on, sweetie-pie," Honey said and laughed. "I wasn't suggesting you get yourself married, just someone to show you around while you're here. What do you think, Taco?"

"I think you should leave her alone and let her find her own guy, Honey," Taco said and swung the truck to a halt outside an elegant suburban house. It was built in the Spanish style with spacious lawns around it. Taco and Honey climbed down from the cab and started to walk across the lawn toward the back of the house where loud music was playing. They didn't even notice that Fiona hadn't gotten out of the truck.

More and more she was wishing that she hadn't come. The tiredness from her long flight was catching up with her, and her thoughts were gloomy. *How could I have been so stupid? I don't even enjoy this sort of thing at home. Nobody wants me here. Taco is using me to tease Honey, and Honey already hates me.*

She wondered if anyone would come looking for her if she stayed in the truck all evening. Just then, Rosie, the Spanish-looking girl from the morning, came from the back of the house. "I thought I heard the truck," she called. "Did you bring the English girl with you, Taco?"

"Sure," Taco said, "she's right here. Fiona?" He turned around, obviously expecting to see her right behind him. "Hey, why are you still in the truck? Come and meet Rosie."

Fiona started to get out of the truck as Rosie hurried over to her. "Oh, Fiona, I'm so glad you've come," she said, grabbing her arms as if they were old friends. "I felt just terrible about this morning. I kept worrying about it all day and wondering what you must think of us for being so mean to you. Especially on your first day here."

As she talked she led Fiona around the side of the house to the backyard. The entire yard was taken up with a large black-tiled swimming pool and a quaint thatched-roof cabana beside it. Torches on poles flickered beside the pool, and a delicious smell was coming from a brick barbecue beside the cabana. About a dozen kids—none of them wearing fancy dresses like Honey—were standing around, listening to a radio and talking. Rosie went right across to the radio and turned it almost off.

"Hey, everybody, listen up," she yelled. Fiona felt herself going crimson with embarrassment as all those faces turned toward her. "I want you all to meet Fiona," Rosie went on. "She comes all the way from England, and she thinks everything here is real weird, so you've got to make her feel at home. Got it?" She bawled this out as a command.

"Yes, ma'am," one of the boys answered, giving her an exaggerated salute. He came across to Fiona, a tall, dark boy whose large eyes gleamed in the light of the torches. "You want a soda, Fiona?" he asked, offering her a can. "My name's Wilt, by the way. I live here."

"Actually none of us are his friends," Rosie quipped. "We just come here because his mom is dumb enough to let us use the pool and the barbecue."

"OK, Rosie," Wilt said. "Now that I know how you really feel about me, all you get are the leftovers."

"Well, on second thought," Rosie said, going over to him, "I guess you're not too bad after all." She leaned over and gave him a tender kiss on the lips. It was quite obvious to Fiona that she was signaling: "This is my special boy. He's not available."

"Now, you go and tend that barbecue, Wilt," Rosie ordered, "and let Fiona and me get to know each other better." And before Fiona could say anything, Rosie had dragged her to a bench beside the pool and away from the other kids.

"Well, I just wanted to say that you're really welcome, Fiona," she said. "I've really been missing Sherry. She and I have always been best friends, and I didn't want her to go. But she asked me to take good care of you and make sure you feel right at home. I'm sure you'll settle in quickly. What grade will you be in?"

"I'm not sure what it's called here for they number all the grades differently," Fiona said. "The same one as Sherry."

"Oh, then you'll be a junior like me," Rosie said. "Most of the kids here are juniors. Taco and Wilt and a couple of the other guys are seniors. Our class is a real neat bunch of kids. They'll make you feel right at home."

"Like this morning, maybe?" Fiona asked with a faint smile.

Rosie patted her hand. "Don't feel bad about that," she said. "We weren't laughing at you. We were laughing because that old horse is so weird," she said. "Princess always did the same thing with Sherry. She just has a thing about water, and nobody can do anything about it, except Taco. Of course, most people don't ride like he does." She looked up at Taco, now dancing with Honey across the pool. "But Taco should have warned you about the horse, then you wouldn't have been scared."

"Yes," said Fiona coldly, watching Taco's strong arms draped around Honey. "He should have warned me, especially after his father told him to put me on Traveler and not Princess. It was a little joke of his to let me think I was riding Traveler."

"Wow, that is really mean," Rosie said. "I wonder why he did it?"

"Oh, he seems to have a million little tricks,"

Fiona said. "Such as telling the cook I liked extra hot chili last night."

"And you don't?"

"I never tasted it before. Luckily I was used to Indian curries in England, so my mouth didn't burn right off, just stung for a few hours!"

Rosie played with her can of soda. The music ended, and the DJ on the radio station did a commercial for the Rancho Steak House. "I wonder what's gotten into him?" she said at last. "He's not usually like that."

"I think it's quite obvious," Fiona said. "He doesn't want me here."

"No, I suppose he wouldn't," Rosie said. "I suppose he wouldn't want any stranger out there. I remember when he was a little kid and the Wests had a student living with them. Taco was pretty mean to him, too."

"But, why?" Fiona asked. "I'm not the sort of person who'll interfere with his life. I'm quiet."

"Well, you see," Rosie said, "since their mother died, Taco and Sherry and their father have been very close. They have Enrique and Maria, and that's it, their own little world. When Professor West went away last year, Taco had to keep the place running with Enrique, which was no small job. He had to do all the ranch chores before he went to school. I guess he's still mad at his father for going away, and now he's mad at Sherry—"

"And at me for taking her place," Fiona interrupted.

The two girls smiled at each other. "Don't worry, he'll get over it soon enough," Rosie said. "Taco has never been slow to appreciate having a cute girl around."

"I noticed that already," Fiona said. Her eyes strayed back to Honey, who was now swaying to the music like some exotic flower. "Are those two a steady couple?" she asked.

Rosie grinned. "She'd like to be, but Taco acts like he doesn't want to get tied down to her. They go around together pretty much, though." Rosie crumpled her can and tossed it into the garbage bin. "He'll give in in the end, of course," she said. "Honey is an only child and very spoiled. She always gets her own way about everything."

She jumped up suddenly. "Excuse me a minute. Wilt's putting the food out, so I'd better give him a hand." And she was gone, her heavy black hair swinging loosely behind her. Fiona watched her go. The last remark had started her thinking. In a way, she was a bit like Honey, an only child who was spoiled and liked to get her own way. Simon had been so easygoing that he went along with whatever she wanted. *Simon!* she thought. *I wish you were here with me now, that you and I were dancing together across the pool. I'd like to tell you how special you really are.*

"Hey, Fiona, over here," Rosie called, motioning her toward the food and thrusting a paper plate into her hand. All of a sudden the others were helping her to all sorts of food. They seemed very friendly and pleased to meet her, asking her tons of questions about life in England, fashions, the latest rock records.

Just as she was taking a bite into her second helping of ribs, a boy came and sat beside her. He was tall and had shiny, dark hair and a build like a football player. "Hi, um, welcome to New Mexico," he said nervously. Fiona wondered for a moment if this was a date Honey had fixed up for her, but then he blurted out, "I'm Richie. I wondered if Sherry gave you a message for me. Um, see, she hasn't written yet. I thought maybe . . ."

Fiona looked at him with surprise. So this was poor faithful Richie whom Sherry had already decided to dump! He was much better looking than she'd imagined. He sat there with such a depressed and serious look on his face that Fiona couldn't help but feel sorry for him. "She told me a lot about you," she said. "And I shouldn't worry about getting a letter. She hasn't even written to her father yet. It's really hard to adjust to a new country. Give her awhile."

Richie's face brightened. "She talked about me?" he asked.

"Several times," Fiona said.

"And did she miss me?"

"She was hardly there long enough to miss anyone yet, Richie," Fiona said tactfully. "But I expect she will soon." Richie smiled. *He has a nice smile*, Fiona thought.

"Well, thanks a lot," he said. "You've taken a load off my mind. It sure is hard when your girlfriend goes so far away." He got up and wandered back to the food table.

Yes, Fiona thought, *it is hard to be far away from the people you love.*

The time change caught up with Fiona around ten o'clock. Rosie found her yawning and told Taco he should take her home. Taco didn't seem to mind, but Fiona suspected that he enjoyed teasing Honey.

"I see you made quite a hit this evening," he said as they climbed into the truck.

"Everyone was so nice," Fiona said. "They really made me feel comfortable."

Taco didn't answer. The truck's headlights cut through the darkness. The engine rumbled softly. Fiona thought about the good food, those juicy ribs and the spicy beans. She thought about Wilt and Rosie and the other kids who'd been so friendly. It was a relief to know that she wasn't going to be a total outsider all year. She found herself slipping into pleasant dreams.

It seemed only moments later that she felt the truck bumping over a rough trail and lurching to a halt. Fiona opened her eyes to find that she had fallen asleep and that her head was resting on Taco's shoulder. Fiona sat up, feeling embarrassed and angry with herself. "I'm sorry," she said stiffly.

"What for?"

"I-I don't want you to think . . ." she stammered.

"Don't worry, I didn't," he said smoothly.

They climbed down from the truck and walked into the house in silence.

Chapter Six

Though Fiona had felt welcome after the party, she soon realized that settling in was not going to be that simple. As soon as she began to feel that she had the hang of life in New Mexico, something else would happen to make her look like a fool again, and Taco would either grin or scowl, depending on his mood. Living with him was such a strain. Since she'd put him down so effectively after their kiss, he only spoke to her when he had to. It was all too obvious that she had wounded his male pride. *But I don't care,* she thought. *He deserved it. He needs to be taken down a peg or two.*

Fiona tried to ignore him, but it wasn't so easy. The trouble was that Fiona and Taco were thrown together so much. They just couldn't escape each other's company. Once school started they drove together every day in the truck.

71

Fiona found school wonderfully relaxing. She was only an exchange student, so everybody expected very little of her. They were pleasantly surprised when she knew something, and nobody minded when she didn't. After years in a high-pressure school where the teachers were constantly giving life-or-death exams, it was a break Fiona really appreciated.

Fiona wrote to Simon a few weeks later:

I keep thinking of you with your three hours of homework every night. We get out of school at two-thirty here and have almost the whole afternoon and evening to ourselves. Sometimes we go over to a friend's house to swim. I am beginning to be useful around the ranch. You probably would not recognize me if you could see me feeding chickens or riding a horse. Although Taco still doesn't think me much of a rider, I can saddle up Traveler by myself and go out on long rides alone. There is so much space here. That's what strikes you most. Wherever you go in England, you can see signs of people. But here there are miles of nothing. You can ride all day and see a hawk and a jackrabbit, maybe, but no roads and no people.

Simon wrote back, letters full of questions. "Taco seems to be creeping into your letters a lot. And what sort of name is that, anyway?"

Fiona smiled as she read his letter and wrote straight back.

Taco isn't his real name, it's Gregory, after his father. I just found that out from his schoolbooks. You see, when he was a little kid, he loved tacos, and he went around saying, "taco, taco." By the way, in case you don't know, a taco is a crispy tortilla stuffed with spicy meat and cheese and lettuce and tomato and hot sauce.

Anyway, to get back to Taco. You really don't have to worry about him because a) he has a beautiful girlfriend named Honey and sees me as a helpless nuisance and b) he is really quite a pain. He thinks that New Mexico is the center of the world and that riding horses and roping cattle are the only worthwhile things in life. Strange, because his father likes to listen to music and read good books. I go more for the cultivated city types myself, did I ever mention that?

Each time she mailed off a letter she realized how far away she was because her letter wouldn't reach England for a week. She tried to make her letters home sound bright and cheerful, even on days when she was feeling down; so she was secretly delighted to see in Sherry's first letter to her that life in London was not all roses for her.

Not that I'm a nasty person, she thought, *and I really don't wish Sherry anything horrible, but Taco thinks I'm quite useless and helpless out here. I must say it's comforting to know that I'm not the only one finding this exchange hard. London is just as strange to Sherry as New Mexico is to me, and all her wonderful western skills are useless in the big city.*

She read through Sherry's letter again. As far as school was concerned, Fiona thought she had gotten by far the best of the exchange. People at Ranch High School could not have been friendlier or more helpful to her. With encouragement from Professor West and Rosie, she had joined the chorus. She liked the relaxed atmosphere, the way teachers chatted with students as if they understood that students were people, too. She liked the way students were allowed to question things and find things out for themselves.

Sherry, on the other hand, was finding out how tough English schools could be.

Where do they find those teachers? I'm sure they were all jailers at the Tower of London before they started teaching. If they ever smiled, their faces would crack. I've only been at school two weeks, and already I've had a fight with every single teacher. Just because I ask a lot of questions, Miss

Fairbotham (what a name!) thinks I'm a troublemaker, and because I didn't want to play hockey when a hurricane was blowing, the gym teacher yelled at me. She told me I'd have to realize that English schools require discipline! And the homework they pile on. If it weren't for Simon, I don't think I'd survive. He's been so sweet, Fiona. He helps me with my homework every night. Especially history, which I'd never understand without him. And he's teaching me to play the guitar, some lovely songs he says you sing together. Oh, and he says to say hi, and he'll write as soon as he gets a dumb report on the French Revolution out of the way.

Fiona had mixed feelings after she read the letter. She was glad that life was not going too smoothly for Sherry. In fact, she wanted to say to Taco, "See how you'd survive in London. You think I'm feeble, but I can get along in rush-hour crowds and play field hockey in a gale!"

But that last bit about Simon unnerved her. She knew she should feel grateful that Simon was being so kind to Sherry, but she didn't. She just felt jealous, then mad at herself for being so. Wasn't Simon going a little too far with his niceness? Did he have to teach Sherry to play the guitar and "their" songs? He didn't have to help her with her homework *every night*.

And that casually tossed-in bit about saying "hi" was the last straw. That her Simon should send her a message through another girl was too much to take. Fiona considered making a play for Richie, just to show Sherry how it felt. But she didn't want Richie—she wanted Simon all to herself, waiting at home for her and feeling lonely and lost.

Because she was feeling upset and abandoned by Simon, Fiona became more frustrated with life in New Mexico. Professor West suggested that it would be good if she learned to drive and volunteered Taco to teach her. Taco made it quite clear that there were a million things he'd rather be doing than teaching some dumb English girl to drive. The first lesson was, therefore, a total disaster. Fiona was scared of the big truck, and Taco couldn't understand why anyone would have to *learn* to drive. He made it seem as if he'd been born knowing how.

"Just put it in gear," he said impatiently, "then take off the hand brake, let the clutch out, and it will go forward by itself. Easy!"

Fiona couldn't even get it into gear. It seemed to require more strength than she had.

"Here," Taco said with a sigh and flicked it effortlessly into first. "Now, let the clutch out slowly."

Fiona's foot came up, and the truck lurched forward and stalled.

"Oh, brother," Taco said, not hiding his

frustration. "We're going to be here all day before she can even get it started."

"Well, I can't help it," Fiona said, halfway between tears and anger. "I've never driven anything before, and this is so big."

"Sherry used to drive it when she was a little kid."

"Well, maybe Sherry was a wonder child, but I'm not," she snapped. "You can just go and tell your dad that I'm hopeless, and there's no point in teaching me."

"Try it again," Taco said, biting each word off, "only take your foot off gently this time and give it a little gas as you do it."

Again the truck jerked forward and stalled.

"What do people drive in England, kiddie cars?" Taco asked sarcastically.

"I think you're a beast!" Fiona shouted. "I don't even want to learn to drive, and if I did want to learn, you are the worst teacher in the entire world." She climbed down from the cab and ran back to the house.

"I hate him, I hate him," she cried out loud to herself. "Who cares about driving stupid trucks and riding stupid horses? Nobody would care a bit about them in London. I've had enough of his laughing at me all the time. I'm just going to ignore him and stay out of his way and not give him anything to laugh at again."

But that resolution was blown the very next morning. Fiona had asked Professor West if she could take over some of Sherry's chores, and he had given her the job of collecting the eggs every morning. The job wasn't quite so easy as it sounded because the chickens never laid their eggs where she expected, and every morning she played a game of hide and seek to find the eggs.

Fiona enjoyed the job. She liked the feeling of being useful. She liked Maria looking up happily as she came in and saying "Oh, good girl" to her. Most of all she liked the early morning air. Before breakfast the air was deliciously cool, and the pale sun threw long black fingers of shadow across the yard. That particular morning she quickly found some of the eggs behind the corral and in the grass beside the road. Then she heard a clucking from the vegetable garden. The vegetables were grown in a little square surrounded by a hedge of prickly pear cactus to keep the cattle out. There was a gate on the far side. Fiona peered between the giant cactus and saw a hen sitting placidly just inside the hedge, within arm's reach.

She lay down and wriggled her arm forward until her hand touched the warm body of the hen. The hen moved off squawking, and Fiona was rewarded with a warm egg. Carefully she closed her fingers around it and brought it back again without touching the giant plants.

"There," she said proudly. "Got it without a scratch."

As she stood up she was aware of a tingling feeling in her arm. She looked down and saw that her arm and hand were covered all over with fine, pin-sized prickles. It looked sort of like a budding porcupine.

"Oh, rats," she said. "Those things are lying all over the ground, and I didn't notice." She tried to brush them off, then to pull them out, but nothing worked. Worse still, her skin was beginning to throb and turn red around each of the spines. Feeling like a big fool, she had to go back into the kitchen for help.

Maria looked up as she came in. "Ah, there she is, my little girl who brings the good eggs for me."

"Yes, but I also got these," Fiona said, showing Maria her prickly hand and arm.

"Ay, ay, ay, Fionacita! How did you do this?" Maria exclaimed.

"I thrust my arm between the prickly pear plants," Fiona said. "I didn't notice that the ground was covered with them."

"Why do you think they use prickly pear to keep out animals?" Maria asked. "Because no animal is dumb enough to try and walk through them. Those little spikes jump into anything that comes near them. You look like a prickly pear yourself. Now what are we going to do with you?"

"I was hoping you'd know that," Fiona said wretchedly. "Do you think I should go and soak in a hot bath? If I have to take them all out one by one with the tweezers, it will take forever."

"A bath won't get these things out," Maria said. "I'd better call Enrique." She opened the window and bellowed for him so loudly that all the chickens in the neighborhood fled, clucking wildly. Enrique came running toward her immediately.

"Take the señorita down to the creek quickly," she said in English, then lapsed into rapid Spanish. Fiona didn't know what was going on, but she followed Enrique. They walked down to the stream, and Fiona stood patiently while Enrique scooped up big handfuls of mud and slopped them all over her arm.

"Now, don't move until that dries," he said. Fiona held her arm still.

"What does this do?" she asked.

"You'll see," Enrique said. "Be patient, please."

Pretty soon the clay dried, making her encrusted arm feel terribly heavy. It was at that moment that Taco came galloping up. With a look of utter delight, he took in the mud-covered arm. "Now what?" he called to Enrique.

"She stuck her arm through the prickly pear hedge," Enrique said.

Taco looked at her in amazement. Fiona could read on his face that he didn't believe anyone could be so dumb. "Boy, we are going to have a job keeping you alive all year," he said. Then he shook his head, urged his horse on, and disappeared.

Enrique took a large stone and cracked open the clay. It peeled off neatly, and, miraculously, the spines were all stuck in it.

"Hey, that's fantastic," Fiona said, feeling much relieved. "Thank you very much. I thought I was going to have to spend the rest of my life covered with those prickles."

"Adobe is good for many things besides houses," Enrique told her. "It takes away swelling from bee stings and insect bites and much more. Now you must hurry, or Taco will leave for school without you."

On the way to school, Taco was still grinning to himself. At last Fiona could bear it no longer. "I suppose you think that I am a complete fool," she said angrily. "Well, let me tell you that at home I can do lots of things very well."

Taco looked across at her and raised one eyebrow. "I didn't know it mattered to you what I thought," he said, his eyes challenging her.

"I don't—" she stammered, unnerved by his blue eyes, "I mean, it doesn't. I mean, I just don't want you to spread it all around the school that I'm an idiot, that's all."

Taco went on smiling to himself. Fiona was now angrier at herself than she was at him. *It's just not fair*, she thought, *because I do care what he thinks.*

Chapter Seven

September slipped into October. The mornings when Fiona went to look for eggs were crisp and chilly. Although the sky was still cloudless each day, there was a hint of fall in the air. Slowly the aspen trees turned into a golden cloak for the upper slopes.

Fiona found that she had fallen into the routine of life on the ranch. She no longer found it strange to get up so early. With all the exercise, her appetite had really picked up, but she could eat more without gaining weight. And she was no longer horrified by the sight of bacon on the same plate with pancakes and syrup. She loved the taste of steak or ribs cooked on the barbecue. She even liked chili, although Maria's extra hot chili still made her eyes water.

At school she got along well with the other kids. She was enjoying chorus, where they sang more modern music than in England, and she had already been given a solo. She hadn't made any special friends, except that Rosie was always extra nice to her. But Rosie was also very popular and on all sorts of committees, so she didn't have much time to spend with Fiona. Still, she didn't mind that much. She hadn't had too many close friends at home in London, either. In fact, Fiona could have tolerated, maybe even enjoyed, the school year quite well if it hadn't been for one thing. And that one thing was Taco. Not that he teased her anymore, or even laughed at her. They had both, by mutual consent, given up trying to teach her to drive. The trouble was that he was there, close by, every day, and Fiona knew that, in spite of herself, in spite of everything she should feel, she was beginning to fall in love with him.

Try as she could, she never managed to get him out of her mind. One day she was looking at her reflection in the mirror. The girl that stared back at her was no longer the white-faced, scrawny girl of two months before. That face now had a thousand freckles on it and a little tan besides, and her hair was streaked with lighter blond strands. Fiona eyed the freckles with disgust, even though everyone else insisted they made her look cute.

"Just my luck," she said. "I get covered in a million freckles, while Taco just gets a beautiful tan!" And then, as she looked in the mirror, she imagined Taco's face joining her own image in the glass. She pictured his blond-streaked hair blowing across his forehead, as it did when he was out riding, and his blue eyes laughing at her from that tanned face.

"Why don't you go away and leave me in peace," Fiona said angrily to the image. "I don't want you at all. I don't even like you. In fact, you are everything I don't like in a boy. You're conceited, you're cocky, you think that the sun revolves around New Mexico and that anyone who can't do what you do is stupid!" She tried to make herself think of Simon, who was warm and gentle and kind, but his image would not come clearly to her. "Is it possible to love and hate a person at the same time?" she longed to ask somebody, but there was no one to ask.

Fiona was tortured every day by having Taco sit beside her at meals, sit so closely in the truck that they were almost touching, yet have him remain distant. Some days she had hope. From the way he looked at her when she wore something special, she could tell he thought she was cute, at least. But that was about all. If he remembered that he had once kissed her, he didn't show it.

Of course, I made it painfully clear that I didn't want him to kiss me again, Fiona thought miserably.

Not that Taco had much time to notice anyone right then. A junior rodeo was coming up, and he planned to win the championship. He was out practicing as soon as it got light every morning and until dark every night. Fiona did not have too clear an idea of what a rodeo was. She knew it was some sort of horse competition and imagined it rather like an English horse show, where people rode around a ring and jumped over gates.

As the day of the rodeo grew closer, the excitement in the West household mounted. Taco was moody and silent; Maria kept urging him to eat more; and Enrique kept giving him unwanted tips on how to win.

They all drove to the rodeo in an ancient Dodge that belonged to Maria and Enrique. Taco had gone ahead very early with the pickup, towing a horse box with Bozo in it. Fiona had been surprised at his selection of Bozo. Bozo was one of the oldest horses on the ranch and had always seemed a plodding old thing to Fiona.

"I didn't know Bozo was good at jumping and things," she ventured in the car.

"He's not," Professor West said. "Taco uses him for the calf roping. You need a steady, dependable horse for that, and Bozo's worked cattle all his life."

"But what will he ride for the other events?" she asked. "He told me he was in three things."

Professor West smiled. "You ride the mount you draw. That would make it too easy if you brought your own horse."

"Bring your own horse to a rodeo, that's funny!" Enrique blurted out, and Fiona was aware that she had said the wrong thing again. *At least not to Taco this time*, she thought gratefully.

By the time they arrived at ten o'clock, the crowd was already densely packed in the bleachers that surrounded a dusty ring. The smell of hot dogs and chili, popcorn and cotton candy competed with the smell of horse. Loud country music blared through every loudspeaker. Everybody except Fiona seemed to know everybody else. And Professor West had to pause with every person they passed and discuss Taco's chances of winning the championship.

"Everybody is allowed to enter three events," Professor West explained to Fiona as they waited for the first event. "Taco chose the bronc and bull riding and the calf roping." At last the music stopped, and the announcer came on the loudspeaker. Then the grand marshal, the sheriff, and their escorts rode into the ring on beautiful horses decked out with rich silver and turquoise harnesses. Next, all the competitors galloped through in a parade, ending with three clowns, who turned cartwheels around the ring.

"Are they to entertain between events?" Fiona asked.

"Much more than that," Professor West explained. "They're the most important part of the rodeo. It's their job to distract a bull to let

86

his rider get to safety. They are all very skilled men. You'll probably have a chance to see them in action."

The first contest was the bronc riding, and Fiona was shocked to see just how different a rodeo was from a horse show at home. A gate opened at one end of the ring, and a horse shot out from it, bucking wildly. The young rider on his back tried to move with the horse, but after about the fourth buck, he was thrown off, and the horse galloped madly around the ring until it was caught. The crowd groaned in disappointment.

"He has to stay on for eight seconds to score," Professor West whispered. Fiona thought privately that it looked impossible for anyone to stay on a horse like that for eight seconds. She also thought that a person would have to be pretty crazy to try. Finally, it was Taco's turn. He shot out on a horse called Crazy Harry. One hand held the strap, and the other waved wildly in the air for balance. He rose and fell with the horse as if he could see into its mind. He made it look so easy that when the buzzer sounded after eight seconds, Fiona was surprised.

"He was fantastic," Fiona said breathlessly.

Professor West nodded proudly. "Yes, he's a wonderful rider."

No one even came close to Taco in the bronc riding and at the end of the event, he strolled over to Fiona and his father. He looked very pleased with himself.

"Nice going, Taco," Professor West said.

"You'll beat them in every event," Maria said, beaming.

"Is Farley Johnson riding today?" Enrique asked shrewdly.

Taco made a face. "Not in the broncs. He chose other events."

"Well, I guess he's going to be the one to beat for the grand championship," Enrique said. "There wasn't too much class in the broncs today."

"I meet him in the calf roping," Taco said, "but that's my best event."

"Come on, we'll walk you over to your horse," his father said, giving him a firm slap on the shoulder.

Fiona hung back, not knowing if she was included in the "we," but Professor West turned around for her. "Aren't you coming, Fiona?" he asked.

Fiona stood by as Taco mounted Bozo. The old horse stood placidly as if the excitement didn't faze him at all. When Taco's name was called, he spurred the old horse on, and Bozo sprang to life. A calf was released into the ring. Bozo galloped alongside it. Taco leaned out of the saddle, grabbed the calf's horns, then flung himself onto the animal, bringing it to the ground with his weight. In seconds his rope flew round all four legs, and the calf was lying helpless on its side. Everyone cheered. Taco came galloping triumphantly out of the ring again.

"I did it!" he yelled, slipping from the saddle. "Two wins out of two, not bad so far, eh?" Then, to Fiona's amazement, he picked her up and spun her around. "It's not every girl who gets riding lessons from the best in New Mexico," he said. Then he seemed to remember something and put her down quickly.

Fiona walked back to her seat in a romantic glow. He'd picked her up in front of all those people, chosen her to share his delight. She could still feel his strong arms around her. The glow lasted until the start of the next event, the girls' barrel racing. One after another, girls rode their horses in and out of a series of barrels, racing against the clock. Fiona, still deep in thought about Taco, hardly paid any attention until the announcer blared out, "Now, Miss Honey Lampert riding Snowman."

Fiona looked up to see Honey come galloping out, dressed all in black on a pure white horse. The horse's bridle was decorated with silver, and so was Honey. Her hatband was silver, as was her belt, and her name was written in silver studs on the back of her shirt. Her long, golden hair looked magnificent, streaming out behind her as she flew around the ring. Snowman moved with such fluid grace that it was almost like watching a river flowing between rocks. They streaked through the course to an easy win.

So, she's a fabulous rider, why should I care? Fiona tried to tell herself. *Taco hugged me when he won.*

The Brahman bull riding was the last event. Taco was one point ahead of Farley Johnson, who had won the lassoing and come in second in the calf roping. As Fiona watched the massive bulls come thundering out snorting and bucking, she felt herself holding her breath in fear. One rider was thrown almost immediately, and the bull turned on him. In an instant the clowns were there, running in front of the fallen rider, waving their extra wide pant legs, pretending to trip over their feet, and all the time skillfully playing with the bull until he got confused and walked sulkily to the side of the ring.

Taco came out on a small red bull. It was incredibly strong, leaping into the air with all four feet at once and trying to turn itself inside out in an attempt to unseat the weight on its back. Taco was flung over to the right. He clung on desperately, slipping farther with each buck. Luckily he managed to hang on until the buzzer sounded. Fiona saw him wipe the sweat from his eyes as he walked back to the gate.

Farley's bull was large and black. It exploded from the gate, taking enormous bucks, which Farley rode easily. Even Fiona could see that he was riding better than Taco had. Then, just at the last second, the bull launched itself sideways and spun around at the same time. Farley went flying off its back and thudded to the ground. He lay still. The bull turned and pawed the ground, ready to charge. One of the clowns came out and had to leap into a barrel as the bull charged him. The second clown drew the bull farther away and also had to hide behind a barrel, which echoed to the thud of the bull's horns. Farley got to his feet and began to stagger toward the fence. A few paces from the fence his legs buckled under him, and he collapsed again. The bull broke away from the clowns and charged straight at Farley. Suddenly Taco leaped down from the gate where he had been sitting and dashed across the ring. The bull swerved and followed him. He launched himself at the fence and just managed to pull himself to safety. Taco climbed back over the fence, and the crowd broke into wild cheering.

Fiona had been so scared that she felt sick. Now she felt very proud. Taco, her Taco, the Taco whose house she shared, had risked his life for his rival. That was the sort of thing you expected a knight in shining armor to do. She began to hurry down to meet him and let him know how she felt. But someone else got there first. While she was still on the steps, Honey and Taco ran toward each other, meeting in a passionate kiss.

"You crazy fool," Fiona heard her say when they finally drew apart. "I thought you'd got yourself killed this time."

"Oh," Fiona said. Tears stung her eyes. She turned away and went back up the steps again before they could see her.

How could she have been so dumb? Fiona wondered as she pushed blindly through the crowd. *Just because he had hugged her when he was feeling good—that didn't mean anything at all. Honey was his girlfriend. How could she ever compete with someone like that? She had everything. She was beautiful, she was a rodeo star, and she was rich. Everything I'm not.* Fiona reflected. *I suppose I'd better face the fact that Taco will never notice me as anything more than the girl who is staying at his house.*

She made a great effort to look interested and pleased while Taco and Honey were awarded trophies. She had to hear, at least a hundred times, what a great couple they made. With great effort, she managed to talk normally all the way home and to help Maria prepare the victory supper. Then, when she finally went to her bedroom, she found a letter on her bed.

From Simon, she thought. *Well, thank heavens someone still cares about me.* She picked it up and went to sit on the bed while she read it. *Dear Simon,* she thought, stroking the envelope tenderly before she opened it.

My dear Fiona,

I know I have been very bad about writing lately, but you know how they pile on homework, and I guess Sherry is giving you all the news anyway. But there was another reason that I haven't written for a while. I wasn't quite sure how to tell you something. It's about Sherry and me. To start with, I looked after her because I knew you wanted me to make her feel at home. But after a while I began to realize how much I enjoyed having her around. I know this is going to come as a shock, Fiona, but I think I've fallen in love with her, and I think she feels the same way about me. I don't want to hurt you, but I thought you would rather know than have us deceive you. You're a good friend, Fiona, and I hope we can still be friends when you come back. Perhaps we relied on each other too much for too long, and perhaps we were both ready for a change.

Fiona gently put the letter down on the bedspread. "Well, that's that," she said. "Now it seems that I have nobody."

Then she cried.

Chapter Eight

Fiona tried very hard to be brave, but her depression did not escape the eyes of the other members of the West household.

"Why aren't you eating?" Maria demanded. "Just when you were beginning to eat like a normal person, you go right back to pecking like a sparrow again."

Professor West went further than that. He cornered her one night after dinner when Tacc was out and Maria and Enrique had gone out for the night, too. "Fiona, is something bothering you?" he asked.

"Bothering me? No, why?" she asked, trying to sound cool and unruffled.

"Because you're spending a lot of time by yourself suddenly and you hardly speak, and I thought you just didn't look happy."

"No, it's nothing," Fiona said. She was no

used to discussing her feelings with adults. *And anyway,* she thought, *I can hardly come out and say I'm hopelessly in love with your son and I hate your daughter for taking my boyfriend, can I?*

"I just wondered if there was anything you'd like to share," Professor West said, walking across the room to pick up a book. "Sometimes problems seem easier when you share them with someone else, and I do want you to think of me as a second father while you're here."

"Thank you, but it's nothing really," Fiona said. "I guess I'm just feeling homesick or something."

"Are the kids at school giving you a hard time?" Professor West asked.

Fiona shook her head, "No, not at all. They're very nice and friendly."

"And my son?" Professor West said, looking up suddenly. "Is he giving you a hard time?"

Fiona felt the blood come rushing to her cheeks. "No, he's not," she said, hoping he wouldn't notice the shakiness in her voice.

"Because it takes Taco awhile to get used to strangers," Professor West went on smoothly. "And he has also been known to break a few hearts. He's a good-looking kid, but he knows it. So I just wondered—?" He looked at her inquiringly.

"There's nothing to wonder," Fiona said. "Taco is fully occupied with Honey Lampert. He certainly can't have been bothering me because he hardly notices I exist."

"Oh," Professor West said, nodding his head wisely. "I see." He got up and smiled at her. "Things always have a way of turning out for the best, you know. Maybe you need a little excitement in your life. I'd better arrange something." And he walked out, leaving Fiona wondering.

She didn't have to wonder long. The next day at dinner Professor West looked across at Taco and said, "I was talking to old Harry Grant today. Seems he's got some wild mustangs corraled up in Bryce Canyon. He wondered if you'd go up and take a look at them sometime, see if there are any worth breaking."

"Sure, Dad," Taco said. "Did he say when he wants it done?"

"Are you free this weekend?" his father asked.

Taco made a face. "Not Saturday. I promised Honey I'd take her into town to see a movie. But I guess Sunday would be all right. What's the big rush?"

"Harry's kind of scared the rains will come and his fences will get washed out," his father said.

"He's got a few weeks yet before he has to start worrying about that. There's no rain forecast yet."

"Well, you know Harry. He's always one for worrying." Taco's father smiled. "Anyway, I promised you'd do it soon, so if you have Sunday free, I suggest you do it then."

Taco shrugged his shoulders. "OK, Dad. You want me to take the truck?"

"It's too far to ride, isn't it?"

"Not if I set out around five or six."

"No, take the truck," his father said. "And why don't you take Fiona along with you. This would be something quite new for her, and she'd get to see some canyon country."

Taco looked across at Fiona, a long, appraising look, and Fiona could tell he was wondering whether she was going to fall into a canyon or get bitten by a rattlesnake or something.

"Oh, that's OK. I'm sure I'd only be in the way," Fiona said.

"No, Fiona, it would be interesting for you to go," Professor West said instantly. "It would do you good to get out and see something, and I know Taco could use the company on the long drive."

"She can come if she wants to," Taco said, "but I want to start real early. It gets hot in those canyons even at this time of year. We'll start as soon as it gets light, OK?"

"OK," Fiona said. A whole day with Taco was not something she was about to turn down. *Not that he really wants me along,* Fiona thought. *I wonder if this was something Professor West cooked up. And I wonder why he cooked it up?*

* * *

They set off Sunday at first light. Maria was up before them and had packed a huge cooler with fried chicken, soft drinks, and fruit.

"Make sure you wear your hat in the sun," the professor said to Fiona. "And don't let my son talk you into doing anything stupid. He knows this country like the back of his hand, and he knows what risks to take. But if something is too hard for you, tell him. And above all, don't become separated. It's very easy to lose your way in the high desert."

"Dad, we're only going out on a little day trip to see some horses," Taco said. "I'm not taking her to discover the lost tombs of the Aztecs or anything."

"Well, just remember that she's a newcomer to this area, Taco," his father said. "You've got to keep an eye on her."

"I know. She manages to get herself into enough trouble right here on the ranch," Taco said. "But don't worry, I'll bring her back safely."

The professor walked them out to the truck. "Harry told me he might come out around midday to join you," he said. "But he also said not to wait for him if he doesn't show up."

"OK, Dad," Taco said. "Now, will you stop worrying? You look like you're sending us on some dangerous mission."

His father smiled. "I just don't want to have

to phone Fiona's parents and tell them we've lost their daughter down a canyon, that's all."

"I have no intention of falling down any canyons," Fiona said. "See you this evening."

The sky was a delicate pearl color as they set off. They drove toward the mountains that were only a purple gray smudge on the horizon. Taco had a country-and-western station blaring out music on the radio. One song followed another, all about suffering women and two-timing men. After a few miles, they turned off the paved road and onto a dusty trail. A sign tacked to the fence said LAZY Y RANCH, HARRY GRANT, OWNER. The truck began to lurch and bump its way over craters and ridges.

Taco turned to Fiona. "I hope you have good shock absorbers," he said. "It's all pretty rough after this."

Fiona, holding on to the armrest, wondered for a moment if she shouldn't have stayed at home. Could she take hours of driving under these conditions? One problem with being skinny was that she wasn't well padded. Those mountains still seemed far way, on the edge of the horizon.

Taco saw her frown. "Don't worry," he said cheerfully. "Everything will be fine if it hasn't rained in the hills yet and washed away part of the trail."

"What happens if it has?" Fiona asked, half

hoping the answer would be that they would have to turn around and go back.

"Then we have the problem of getting the truck through a riverbed," Taco said.

I think he's just saying that to scare me, Fiona thought. "Well," she said out loud, "your father said that Harry Grant was up there last week, so if it hasn't rained since then, we're all right."

"Smart girl," Taco said and grinned. "Except that I bet he went up on his horse. He hates using a car or truck unless he really has to."

"Who do these horses that he's trapped belong to?" Fiona asked.

"Nobody yet. They're wild, and they're on his land, so he'll take his pick. Maybe he'll let me buy one if I like the look of it."

"I should think you have enough horses," Fiona said.

"I could never have enough horses," he answered. "Anytime I see a new horse who looks like he'd be a challenge to break, I've just got to have him."

"Then you'll end up with far too many horses."

Taco shook his head. "I usually sell them after I've broken them. I lose interest once they're tamed."

They drove on. The country-and-western station petered out into static crackle. Taco switched it off.

"Too far from town now, I guess," he said.

Far in the distance, on their left, Fiona could see a line of trees that marked the entrance to a ranch house. Then, beyond it, nothing, just gray scrub stretching toward red hills.

"Does Harry Grant own all this?" she asked in wonder. In England farms were little affairs, fields bordered by hedges with a few cows or neat rows of crops. She had never imagined one farm stretching as far as the eye could see in all directions at once.

"Yup," Taco said as if it were the most normal thing in the world.

"He must be very rich."

"Not really. You need a lot of land out here to graze cattle. There's not much water this side of the Rio Grande. He probably only grazes one cow per acre out here."

As they drove, the sun came up full over the eastern hills, and the whole valley suddenly flamed with bright color. Fiona could see that the hills ahead, which had looked as if they were a uniform, dark brown color, were banded with red and orange rock, sliced with deep canyons and gorges.

The truck bucked and lurched like a bronc over the rocky trail. Fiona now needed to hold on with both hands to stop herself from being flung about.

Taco stopped to consult a hand-drawn map he carried in his pocket. "Let's see," he said, peering around. "Bryce Canyon should be directly across the arroyo. Can you see any sign of an arroyo yet?"

"What, in plain English, is an arroyo?" Fiona asked. "You forget I'm the newcomer you have to take care of."

"Sorry," he said and smiled. "An arroyo is a gully that fills up with water when there's a flash flood. It's a dry riverbed most of the year."

"Well, there's a line of bushes over to the right," Fiona said. "Could that be it?"

"Good thinking," he said and turned the truck. The wheels screamed as they bounced over scrub. The bank of the arroyo was a steep, red sand cliff, and they had to drive along it for a long way before they found a place low enough to cross. Even so, it was a bone-shaking crossing.

"It's hard to believe that water can carve such a deep channel if it comes through only once or twice a year," Fiona said.

Taco nodded. "You have to see it to believe it. When there's a storm high in the mountains, it comes rushing down with such a force that it can sweep away trucks."

"Heavens," Fiona said, looking around worriedly for dark clouds lurking over the mountain tops.

"It's all right. There's no rain forecast today," Taco said. "You can sit back and enjoy yourself."

Suddenly Fiona realized something. She and Taco were having a normal conversation. No sarcastic comments, no put-downs. Well, that was one step in the right direction, she thought happily. Maybe there *was* some hope after all.

Taco drove right up to the first line of hills and entered a long, narrow valley. Rocks towered high on either side. He had to steer around giant boulders, obviously brought down in storms. At last he brought the truck to a halt beside an overhanging cliff.

"We'll have to walk from here," he said. "Even this truck won't make it any farther."

They got out, and Fiona was struck by the total silence she'd felt so often in New Mexico. Just the barest sigh of a breeze blew through the crags; otherwise, no sound at all. The sound of their feet on the loose rock seemed to be magnified into giants' footsteps. Taco grabbed a coil of rope from the back of the truck and swung it onto his shoulder.

"You're not thinking of bringing some wild horse back with you, are you?" Fiona asked in horror.

Taco grinned. "You never know when rope might be useful," he said. He bent to pick up the cooler. Fiona offered to take one handle, and he willingly let her. Swinging it between them, they made their way up the canyon to where a crude fence had been built right across the valley floor. It was an ideal spot to trap horses. The canyon walls were impossibly steep, and the valley came to an abrupt end after about a mile. Whoever had built the fence had also put an oil drum full of water beside it.

"Move very quietly from now on," Taco said softly. "We want to get right up to the horses. Oh, and don't whisper. Whispering spooks wild animals. Just talk naturally in a low voice if you have to say something."

They left the cooler under a stunted tree that threw a small pool of shade onto the parched earth. Then they set off, Taco leading and Fiona several paces behind. Now that she had reached this stage, she wasn't exactly sure she wanted to come face to face with a herd of wild horses. What if they attacked? What if they were frightened and stampeded right at her?

The floor of the valley climbed sharply upward. The ground underfoot was studded with sharp rocks that cut through the soles of her sneakers. When a lizard darted out from a rock beside her foot, she barely managed to stifle a scream.

Taco strode ahead, looking around, almost testing the wind like a wild animal himself. Fiona noticed how silently he moved while she managed to step on every dry twig or loose rock in the valley.

How at home he looks, Fiona thought.

Suddenly Taco froze in his tracks and turned, putting a finger to his lips. Then he pointed to a group of gnarled old trees.

At first Fiona could see nothing. Then she was able to make out five horses standing in the dappled shade, their coats blending in perfectly with the surroundings. They were standing head to tail to keep the flies off one another, and they appeared relaxed, as yet unaware of the presence of strangers.

"I'm going closer," Taco said in a low voice. "I want to get a good look at them. You can follow behind me if you don't make too much noise." He moved off silently and quickly, seeming to melt from rock to rock, from shadow to shadow as if he were part of the landscape.

Fiona stayed where she was. *I can see quite well enough from here,* she said to herself, *and if I follow him, I'm bound to trip over something and make them all run away.*

After a while Taco came back to her. "There's a fine stallion among them," he said. "He looks young and strong. I hope Harry doesn't want him. There are a couple of foals, too, just a few months old. Maybe I'll take one of them if I don't get the stallion. You want to come and take a look?"

Fiona could hardly refuse this time. She followed Taco up the side of the canyon, moving from rock to rock until she was directly above the horses and could look down on them. As well as the five larger ones she had been able to see from a distance, there were two sweet babies with soft golden coats. Taco was right about the stallion—he was magnificent. His coat was a wonderful light gold color, and his mane was almost silver. He looked like a horse out of Greek mythology, fit for carrying a hero. Fiona moved to get a better view, and a trickle of loose gravel cascaded down. At once the stallion looked up, aware of them. He snorted in alarm and began to drive the mares and foals ahead of him down the valley.

"Come on," Taco said, jumping down from the rock. "We'll get a much better look at them in the open country down by the fence." He began to hurry after the disappearing horses.

"But won't it be dangerous if you corner them at the fence?" Fiona asked.

Taco smiled proudly. "I've never yet met a horse I couldn't handle," he said. "I've been roping wild horses since I could stand. In fact, if you'd like, I'll give you a demonstration of how easy it is to rope a wild mustang."

"But you're not strong enough to hold a horse like that," Fiona blurted out. *Oh, no, I've said the wrong thing,* she thought.

But Taco didn't seem to notice. "I'll use the fence to take the strain. It's easy," Taco said. He uncoiled the rope from his shoulder and strode off after the horses. Fiona wished she could stop him, but she knew that anything she said right then would only urge him on to more and more daring acts.

"See, there he is," Taco said, pointing to the place where the fence met the cliff. "He's smart, trying to find a way out, but he can't jump anything that high."

The horses looked up with frightened eyes as Taco walked toward them. The mares and foals crowded behind the stallion. He didn't attempt to run but stood solidly on all four feet, ears alert and ready to do battle. Taco walked calmly toward him. When he was still a fair distance from the horse, he flung out the rope. It sailed through the air, and the noose fell cleanly over the horse's neck. Fiona had to admit it was a wonderful throw.

The mustang didn't hesitate for a second. He reared and plunged like a mad thing. Taco, holding the rope tense, moved down toward the fence, ready to make the rope fast to one of the thick posts. Then, without warning, the stallion changed tactics. He sprang forward, rearing up and lunging at Taco. Taco tried to move out of the way, but he was trapped between the stallion and the fence. The powerful hooves lashed out at him. He saw the blow coming and dodged to avoid it, so that instead of having his face struck, he was kicked on the shoulder. He cried out in pain and slumped against the fence. The stallion saw his chance and made a break for freedom. The great beast streaked away, and Fiona watched in horror as Taco was jerked off his feet and dragged behind it, the rope wound around his wrist.

Chapter Nine

Until then Fiona had watched the whole thing as if she were not part of it. As Taco was dragged away, however, she lurched into action.

"Taco!" she screamed, running in a hopeless attempt to stop the escaping horse. Of course, she wasn't fast enough, and her ankles twisted as she tripped on the sharp rocks. All the time a little voice inside kept telling her it was hopeless, that Taco would be dead by now, that she might as well stop running. But still she stumbled on. She could feel tears running down her cheeks and hear sobs escaping from her throat. But she was like a robot, programmed to chase that horse until it released Taco, and she wasn't going to stop until it did.

She found him not far up the valley. The rope had either worked itself free or snapped against a sharp rock because the horse had vanished and Taco was lying quite still on the red earth. She didn't stop to wonder what she would find. She ran forward and dropped to her knees beside him. There was blood trickling down his face and arms. His clothes were ripped. His eyes were closed.

"Oh, Taco," she pleaded out loud. "Please don't die."

Still he didn't move. She put her face down close to his and felt a faint breath on her cheek.

What do I do now? she asked herself, feeling her heart thudding so loudly that it should have echoed back from the cliffs. *I'm not strong enough to lift him. Besides, I shouldn't move him in case he's broken something.*

"I'll get some water," she decided out loud. "At least I can stop the bleeding." She ran back to the fence and soaked her scarf in the rain barrel. Then she brought a can of orange soda from the cooler and hurried back to Taco. The sun beat down, and two large birds wheeling above in the sky looked suspiciously like vultures. Fiona had a horrible vision of a great flock of vultures descending silently, sitting all around Taco and waiting. She made herself hurry back to him again even though her side hurt and her legs felt like jelly.

Taco still hadn't moved. Fiona bent down to make sure he was still breathing. She wondered if she could remember anything of her artificial respiration course if he wasn't.

"Fiona?" a voice barely whispered in her ear.

"Oh, Taco, you're not dead," she cried.

"What happened?"

"The horse kicked you, then you got dragged after it," she said, looking down at him with concern and gently wiping the blood from his face.

"I was just about to say I felt like I'd been dragged by a wild horse." He managed a weak smile but winced with pain.

Once his face had been cleaned up, the cuts didn't look as dreadful as Fiona had feared. They were mostly long scratches, which were bleeding a lot but weren't deep. Taco's face was battered and bruised, and one eye was swollen almost shut. Fiona was very conscious of the hot sun beating down on them.

"Do you think you could move?" she asked. "I'm sure it's not good for you to lie in the sun like this."

Taco tried, then grimaced in pain. "I can't move my right shoulder and arm at all," he said. "And it hurts to breathe. I think I must have broken some ribs as well as the arm."

"Then I'd better bring the shade to you," Fiona said. She went over to the nearest tree and managed to break off some small branches. These she stuck in the ground around Taco as a crude screen.

"I'll go back to the truck and get my jacket to put over them in a minute. Then you'll have some proper shade," she said. "Would you like a sip of orange soda? I brought a can."

"Thanks," he said wearily.

Fiona lifted his head gently and trickled the liquid into his mouth. After a few gulps he lay back exhausted and closed his eyes.

"Listen, Taco," she said. "I've got to get help. What can I do?"

He opened his eyes again. "You could try the CB radio in the truck," he said, forcing the words out one by one. "One-nine is the band you'd get someone on. Just say, 'Breaker one nine, emergency.' But I think we may be out of anyone's range."

"OK. I'll be right back," she said.

He didn't answer, so she hurried back down to the truck. She had seen Taco use the CB radio a couple of times, but she had never paid much attention to how it worked. Now she looked at the row of buttons in panic.

"Relax, Fiona," she told herself firmly. "Just tackle it calmly and logically. Look for the on/off switch first, there must be one." She flipped a lever and was rewarded with a burst of static crackle. The channel selector was already on one-nine. Nervously she picked up the microphone as she had seen Taco do. "Breaker one-nine, breaker one-nine, emergency," she began. The crackle continued just as loudly. "Oh, rats, there must be a button for talk and receive." She looked around and found it on the microphone. She flicked into the talk mode and tried again. "Breaker one-nine, emergency. Breaker one-nine, emergency. Come in, anybody. Help." She flicked back—only static. Even when she adjusted the fine tuning, there was no hint of an answering voice, only louder or softer crackle.

Sighing, she flipped it off again, then climbed down from the truck with her jacket and Taco's, too. She made her way back to him. He was more awake now and looked over to her as he heard her footsteps.

"Any luck?" he asked.

She shook her head. "Only static."

He sighed. "I thought so. We must be miles out of range. I just hoped someone might be driving in the hills."

"What about Harry? Didn't your father say he'd be out later?"

"He said he might," Taco agreed. He coughed painfully. "You know, you take breathing for granted until it really hurts."

"Is there anything I can do to make it better?" Fiona asked. "I daren't move you too much."

"My lips are dry again," he said. "Give me another sip of soda." The can was covered with ants, and Fiona brushed them off. Taco took a few sips, then closed his eyes in exhaustion. Fiona tried to arrange the jackets to make more shade, then sat beside him, waiting.

The sun beat down. Fiona had never felt so totally alone. The rocks glowed bright red. A huge bird of prey soared out from the cliff, hung motionless against the sky, and then plunged down to earth only to glide up again with something in its claws. A relentless line of ants kept trying to make their way toward Taco; Fiona had to head them off every few minutes.

What if Harry doesn't come? she thought, drawing a pattern in the red dust with her finger. Taco was clearly in a bad way, drifting in and out of consciousness. Would he survive a night out here? Nobody would know they were missing until that night, and it would be impossible to find them in the dark.

The sun began to dip toward the west. Fiona adjusted the shade for Taco. He moved his undamaged hand and touched hers gently. "Fiona, you're a great girl," he said in a cracked whisper. "I'm sorry for everything."

"Nothing to apologize for," she said. "I was a tenderfoot. Now I'm getting broken in a bit."

He smiled. "The hard way," he said. "What time is it? My watch got wrecked by that horse."

"It's nearly three."

"I don't think Harry is going to come," he said. He gave a long sigh. "I don't feel like lying here all night. There are rocks digging into me, and I'm beginning to feel cold."

Fiona felt herself trembling as she realized what she had to do. It was something that had been lurking in the back of her mind, something she had kept back there because she dreaded it so much. She swallowed, then forced herself to say, "I'll take the truck and drive for help."

He looked at her, his eyes very bright. "You couldn't do it," he said. "You know what your attempts at driving were like, and you wouldn't find the way. If you went off course, you could be lost for days."

"Then what do you suggest?" she snapped, angry that he should be voicing her own fears out loud. "It gets cold at night. We can't just stay here, waiting for someone to find us!"

Then she looked at him, no longer the strong one who laughed when she couldn't keep up with him, and her heart melted. She reached over and touched his hand. "I think I can do it, Taco. I might not use the right gears, but I think I can get it going. And all I have to do is follow our tracks back. Even if I lose them, the sun is pointing west, so I just have to keep that in my eyes. I'll meet a road eventually."

His hand gripped hers. "All right," he said. "The key is in my jacket pocket. But take care, Fiona."

"Don't worry, I'll be back with help as soon as I can," she said. Then she leaned down and gave him a little kiss on the cheek.

"I thought you said you wouldn't kiss me if I were the last boy on earth." Taco gave her a weak smile.

"That was purely a professional kiss, nurse to patient," she said.

"I think I'll wait until I feel a bit better for the unprofessional one," he said. "It wouldn't be wise to raise my pulse right now."

"I'll hurry back," she whispered. Then she got up and walked toward the truck, trying to look confident and not show her terror. The cab felt stiflingly hot, and the leather seat burned through her jeans. Her fingers were trembling so much that she couldn't get the key into the ignition. She remembered all too clearly that driving lesson when she had stalled the engine and Taco had yelled. Now she would have willingly traded a yelling Taco for the empty loneliness of that cab. She turned the key and put her foot on the gas pedal. The powerful engine roared to life. "Clutch in, shift into first," she said out loud, "hand brake off." The truck lurched forward, and she managed to get it turned around.

"Well, what do you know," she said, amazed that the great monster had so far obeyed. "Now let's just see if I can keep it going until we get somewhere."

The big truck bumped its way down the trail. Fiona was concentrating so hard on following the tire tracks on the dry earth that she couldn't manage to shift up to second gear. The engine screamed and groaned alarmingly. She only hoped Taco wouldn't hear. The steering wheel

115

in her hands seemed like a live thing, struggling to wrench itself from her hands and run her into a rut she couldn't get out of. The sun, sinking in the west, glared straight into her eyes. She would have lowered the sun visor, but again her fingers didn't dare leave the wheel. Worse still, what looked like a heavy bank of dark clouds seemed to be gathering above the western hills. Taco certainly wouldn't last the night if there was a storm. She gripped the wheel harder and pressed her foot on the gas pedal, willing the truck forward.

At last the hard, dark line of the arroyo appeared. Fiona felt her back damp with sweat and felt wet drops run down her face as she inched the truck down the steep bank. She felt it starting to run away with her, and she panicked and jammed on the brake. The truck reached the bottom and lurched to a halt; the engine stalled. The complete silence seemed to beat menacingly in on Fiona. She turned the key again. "Start, please start," she begged. The engine coughed, turned over, and faded out again.

What's wrong? What am I doing wrong? If only I knew how engines worked, she thought. *It can't have run out of gas, can it?* The high sides of the arroyo rose above the truck, throwing a shadow onto Fiona. She remembered that bank of clouds and the way a dry gulley could fill up in moments in a flash flood.

She turned the key again and pushed the gas pedal flat on the floor. The motor whined and screamed in protest. The engine turned over; the truck lurched forward and stalled again.

"Rats, I left it in gear," she said, shifting to neutral.

On the third try the truck sprang to life. Fiona shifted into first and put her foot down hard on the gas petal. Mistake! She could feel the back wheels spinning in the soft sand. Visions of being trapped, sinking deeper and deeper into the riverbed made her feel panicky again. "Not so hard this time," she told herself, trying to calm down. "Just ease it forward gently."

That time she barely touched the pedal and felt, to her great relief, the truck begin to move forward slowly. Up the far bank it went, and she was free. The arroyo was behind her. In less than an hour she brought the truck to a rather undignified halt outside Harry Grant's ranch house, and before darkness fell, a team of men had carried Taco out of Bryce Canyon on a stretcher and driven him to the hospital.

Harry Grant drove Fiona home in the truck, for which she was very grateful. After her struggle with the truck, she felt suddenly overcome with tiredness. In the hustle that followed, it seemed that everyone had forgotten about her. Professor West and Maria rushed around grabbing things to take to the hospital, then disappeared, leaving Fiona all alone. Although her stomach was growling with hunger, she couldn't bring herself to do more than nibble at some bread and cheese, then go to bed. As soon as her head touched the pillow, she collapsed in a deep sleep.

The next morning Fiona learned how quickly news spreads in a small community. Professor West, looking rather red-eyed after a night at the hospital, drove her to school. As soon as she entered the building, she was instantly surrounded by a group of students, some of whom she didn't even know.

"How's Taco? Is he going to be OK? Is it true he was dragged by a wild horse?"

Fiona answered all their questions patiently, trying to give the facts and not make them sound too dramatic, trying not to brag about her part in the rescue.

"I hear you're the big heroine," Wilt said. He turned to the others. "The doctor said Taco would have died if it hadn't been for her."

"What did she do?" a couple of newcomers asked.

Feeling all those eyes on her, Fiona curled up her toes in embarrassment. "Oh, she was terrific," Wilt said. "She gave him first aid, and then she drove all the way down to Harry Grant's place in the truck when she doesn't even know how to drive!"

Pretty soon it was all around school, and Fiona was becoming known as the girl who saved

Taco West. It was embarrassing to be stared at and whispered about, but it felt good, too. At least, it felt a lot better than being pointed out as the newcomer, the girl who made funny mistakes.

At lunchtime Professor West showed up on campus and sought her out. "If you aren't busy, Taco's asking to see you," he said. "I told him I'd pop you down during your lunch period. Then the whole family can visit after school."

A rather pale and very battered-looking Taco was lying in a private room when Fiona went in. One arm, from shoulder to fingers, was in plaster and resting outside the white sheet. His eyes were closed when she tiptoed in. He opened them, focused on her, and his face lit up in a smile.

"Oh, hi," he said. "I'm glad you came."

"How are you feeling?"

"Not bad at all now. They've given me so many shots I feel like a pincushion."

"I see you did break your arm," she said. "What else did you do?"

"Apart from making a fool of myself?" he asked and gave her such a gentle smile that she thought her heart would melt. "I broke a couple of ribs and got bruises you wouldn't believe where. Oh, and dislocated my shoulder. But the doctor told me I was very lucky."

"You were. When I saw that horse drag you away, I expected to find you smashed to a pulp."

119

"It's funny," Taco said, looking out of the window to where a bright red maple tree was stirring in the gentle wind, "but I don't remember any of it. I remember lassoing the horse and then realizing he had me trapped as he reared up. But that's all I can remember until you were washing my face. And you know what else is funny? As I was coming to, I thought it was my mother washing my face. I always used to hate it when she did that, and I was about to say 'Cut it out, Mom,' when I remembered."

Fiona smiled. "So that's how you think of me, like a second mother? Well, I suppose it could be worse."

Taco's eyes looked alarmingly bright against the whiteness of his face and the crisp hospital sheets. "I don't think of you like that at all," he said. "And the weirdest thing is that I haven't even dreamed about my mother for years. I guess you have the same sort of gentle hands, and you made me feel safe when I was scared, like she used to."

He looked away as if he were ashamed of being so emotional. She saw then, for the first time, that Taco was only tough on the outside. He had to hide his hurts because there was no one around to make them better. Fiona longed to reach down and put her arms around him, but she didn't dare.

"I want to tell you something, Fiona," he said, still looking away from her. "That's why I asked

Dad to bring you in right away. It was some-thing I had to tell you. When I was lying out there all alone after you'd gone, I started to worry—not that you wouldn't come back or that I would die, but about you! I kept thinking, what if she turns over the truck or it runs away with her or she goes in the wrong direction and gets lost? I suddenly realized how terrible it would be if anything happened to you."

There was a silence. A bird landed on the maple branch outside, fluffed out its feathers, and gave a high-pitched peep.

"Fiona?" he asked. "Do you still mean what you said that time?"

"About what?"

"You know, about not wanting me even if I was the last boy on earth?"

"I never did," she said. "I wanted you to like me from the first moment we met. I was hurt because I knew you were only making fun of me."

There was another silence, broken only by the sound of dishes rattling as a cart was wheeled by in the hallway.

"It's dumb, isn't it?" he said at last. "We've wasted so much time. I didn't want you to come. I thought you'd look down on us, coming from a big city like London. I didn't want you laugh-ing at us, so I guess I tried to get the laugh on you first."

"Well, you succeeded," she said.

"I'm sorry," he said again. "I take everything back. I thought you were a soft, helpless city girl who didn't belong in our world. I was wrong. I don't know many girls who could have done what you did yesterday."

"Taco, I have to go," she said, not knowing how to handle his praise any more than his jokes. "I shall be late for class."

"Sure," he said. "Will you come back after school?"

"If you want me to."

"I want you to. And I want to ask you something. Can we start again when I get out of here? I mean, pretend like we just met?"

Fiona smiled. "If you like," she said. "Although I have my suspicions that all those shots have made you sentimental. When you get back home, I bet you'll revert to your normal, wicked self."

He grinned. "Probably," he said. "But my normal, wicked self can be a lot of fun, too! Bye, Fiona."

"Bye, Taco."

Chapter Ten

Taco was in the hospital almost two weeks. Fiona went to see him every day. With each visit she noticed an improvement in his condition, and the quiet, emotional, thoughtful Taco soon started to return to the restless wisecracker. Each day the nurses had more trouble with him, complaining that he tried to do too much, that he wouldn't rest or take his medicine. Finally, at the end of two weeks, they were all glad to see him go home.

Fiona, in a way, was sad. She had come to treasure those visits, alone in the little white room with Taco. The room had been a private place where they could talk about things they would never talk about anywhere else, and she felt that they had finally gotten to know each other.

Some of Taco's school buddies had gone to

visit him, too, but not Honey. For the first few days Taco didn't even mention Honey's name. Fiona was torn between feeling relieved that he hadn't wanted to see her and wondering if she should suggest that Honey see him. She sorted out those feelings finally when Honey stopped her in school one day.

"How's my Taco feeling these days?" she asked as she met Fiona in the hall.

Fiona resented her calling him "my" Taco. "He's doing just fine, thank you," she said politely.

"Well, tell him to hurry and get out of that hospital!" Honey said.

"He's hurrying as fast as he can," Fiona said. "Why don't you go and see him sometime?"

Honey looked shocked. "Me? Go to a hospital? I hate the places. They give me the creeps. All those sick folks lying about. No, you tell him I'll come over and see him when he gets home again. Oh, and you can give him a big kiss for me!"

"With pleasure," Fiona said and noticed the way Honey stared at her as she walked away.

That evening she delivered the message. "Honey says I have to give you this," she said, leaning across to kiss his cheek.

Taco looked surprised and pleased. "Now who was that supposed to be from?" he asked.

"I was only passing on the message from Honey," she said.

"Well, in that case, Honey doesn't bother with kissing cheeks," he said. "She's always much more direct." Taco grabbed Fiona's wrist, and what might have happened next was interrupted by an aide.

"Anyway, where is Honey when I need her?" Taco asked, his eyes challenging Fiona as the aide changed his water jug.

"She said she doesn't like hospitals," Fiona answered.

Taco grunted. "She doesn't like anything that's inconvenient to Miss Honey Lampert," he said. "If she'd been with me up in Bryce Canyon, she would have gone home without me."

That conversation made Fiona feel quite hopeful.

Taco came home from the hospital in time for Thanksgiving. His arm was still in a cast, and he walked with a slight limp, but he was, as Fiona predicted, back to his old, wicked self. He couldn't ride or do much around the house, so he bugged everybody else, telling Maria how to cook and Enrique how to run the ranch. To Fiona he was different, but not in the way she had hoped. He treated her almost as if he were her big brother. But Fiona didn't want a brother. Living in the same house and being constantly around each other made it very hard to step across the barrier between friend and boyfriend. They rarely had a chance to be alone without

Maria or Taco's father walking in, and even if they were alone, there was a certain shyness between them.

Right after Taco got home, a letter came for Fiona from Sherry. It was the first she'd heard from Sherry since Simon's confession, and she looked at it suspiciously.

Just at that moment, Taco walked into the room. "Don't tell me my sister has finally decided to write someone," he said. "I thought she was lost forever on a London subway. What does she say?"

"I don't know. I haven't opened it yet."

"Well, read it out loud so we can both laugh," he said. "I don't know why you're the one who gets written to. Come on, open it."

Fiona was not eager to read the letter out loud. Nobody else in the family knew about Sherry and Simon, and Fiona didn't want them to know. But Taco was in a playful mood and looked as if he might steal the letter from her at any minute, so she opened it and started to read.

"Hi there, Fiona!

I haven't written for so long because I was a bit shy about writing to you after you-know-what happened."

"What does she mean by that?" Taco interrupted.

126

"It's personal," Fiona said.

"OK, go on reading," Taco commanded.

"I hope you're having a great time in New Mexico. I would be having a great time here, too, if it weren't for all this homework every night. And the cold! I thought it got cold in New Mexico in the winter, but it's not the same sort of cold. Ours is dry, and I guess that doesn't feel as cold as the English kind. I can tell you quite honestly that I have never felt so cold in my life. Your father calls it a mild morning, and I'm wearing knit tights and two sweaters! Thank goodness for hot water bottles. I take one to bed with me every night. I'm also learning how to get dressed in bed. Talk about survival skills.

Simon is being so sweet. He's taken me to all sorts of places I'd never have gone without him, and he—"

Fiona stopped reading. "She doesn't write much else," she said, folding up the letter.

Taco reached across and took it from her.

"Hey, come on, Taco, that was written to me," she said as she made a grab for the envelope. He held her off with his good arm and managed to glance through the rest of the page before releasing her.

"So who is this Simon?" he asked.

127

Fiona looked away. "He used to be my boy-friend."

"Oh, I get it—and Sherry stole him."

"Sort of."

"Does it still matter to you?" he asked quietly.

She looked up and met his eyes. "I suppose it still hurts my pride," she said.

"But it doesn't break your heart?"

"No, not anymore," she admitted.

"I didn't think so," he said and smiled. "We're an annoying family on the whole, aren't we?"

"Very annoying. Now, let me have my letter back," she said, snatching it from him and darting away before he could catch her.

It was strange to Fiona how early Americans began preparing for Christmas. Here it was only early December, and already there were Christmas specials on TV. The shopping malls were hung with giant snowflakes and candles, and "Rudolph, the Red-Nosed Reindeer" boomed out from loudspeakers. In England Fiona had always done her shopping on Christmas Eve. She had loved the feel of the streets crowded with busy shoppers, the carol singers on the corners, the turkeys hanging in butcher shop windows, and the Christmas trees propped up against the greengrocer shops.

"Americans are so funny," she said to Taco one evening. "They prepare for Christmas so far ahead. All the Christmas things were in the stores back in November, and most people have already done their shopping. The shopping malls never seem to be very busy."

Taco nodded. "That's what you call commercialism. You should see the little kids who come to see Santa. They have a list of things a mile long of everything they want, all the toys they've seen in TV commercials."

"Well, I had better get something for my parents soon," Fiona said.

"I know a place where you can buy beautiful turquoise jewelry," Taco said. "These Zuni Indians make it on their reservation. It's quite expensive but absolutely worth it. We could drive out there if you want."

"So long as I don't have to drive," she said and grinned.

"I thought you did pretty well," he said.

"You weren't there to see me, thank goodness. I got the truck back safely, but that was positively my last driving experience in the USA."

"Maybe Dad can drive us out there tomorrow," Taco said. "He likes going out there because he knows all the people. The Zunis are one of the tribes he studies."

The next day was beautiful, as sunny and warm as an English summer, and Professor West was happy to drive to the reservation. In the front yards, flowers were still blooming.

"Maybe that's why I don't feel more Christmasy," Fiona said. "The weather is still like summer."

"It can change quickly here," Professor West said. "Wait until you wake to a foot of snow."

"Too bad I won't be able to help out with the cattle when it does snow," Taco said. "I just can't get my cast wet."

"Yes, it is too bad," his father quipped back. "You also won't be able to go skiing this winter."

"Don't remind me," Taco muttered. "Do you think my shoulder will be strong enough by spring vacation?"

"Only if you exercise it properly by doing lots of work around the ranch," his father said and winked at Fiona.

Fiona had expected something pretty exotic from an Indian reservation, so it was rather a letdown when the professor pulled up outside a very modern house trailer complete with TV antenna. A dark-skinned girl wearing designer jeans and a bright red sweatshirt came out when she saw them get out of the car.

"Oh, hi there, Professor," she called, waving cheerfully. "I'll go get Dave. He's out helping them with the generator over at the motel."

"Don't worry, Celia," Professor West said. "We just came to see the jewelry. This is our house guest from England, and she wants to send home some presents to her folks."

The girl smiled at Fiona. "Sure, come on in. I've got some nice pieces right now." She opened

130

a door to an office at one end of the trailer. Then she produced tray after tray of beautiful silver pieces. Fiona was immediately drawn to a necklace that Professor West told her was called a squash blossom. But since it cost over two hundred dollars, she chose things smaller and cheaper, a pair of cuff links for her father and a ring for her mother.

After she'd paid for them, Taco was still standing and examining a bracelet. It was very unusual, made of rows of turquoise and coral with silver.

"What do you think of this?" he asked.

"Very pretty," she answered.

"Yeah, I thought so, too," he said and put it back.

Fiona took her purchases and walked back to the truck with Taco. "Oh, hold on a second, Fiona," he said. "I forgot to ask Celia something."

I wonder if he went back for that bracelet? Fiona couldn't help thinking. *Could it possibly be for me?*

That warm feeling of imagining Taco was going to give her the lovely bracelet lasted until school Monday morning when Honey came up to her in the girls' bathroom.

"I hear you went out to the Zuni Reservation on Saturday," she said casually. She took out a brush and began to comb her flowing hair. "Tell me something—Taco didn't by any chance buy a bracelet, did he?"

131

"I've no idea," Fiona said, feeling herself going red.

"Because I've been dropping hints to him for the longest time that I wanted a Zuni bracelet." She smiled at herself in the mirror. "I hope he's finally taken the hint. I'm getting very bored with the way he's been neglecting me lately. Of course, I know he hasn't been able to drive, which is a real bore. In fact, I'm going to the Christmas dance with Billy Peterson because I can hardly dance with a guy who's got his arm wrapped in plaster."

She finished brushing her hair then swept it back with two jeweled combs. "One good thing," she said. "A guy with a plaster cast can hardly cheat on me, can he?"

Fiona felt herself getting hotter and more angry. Finally she exploded. "I've met some nasty people in my life," she said, "but you really take the cake. How many times did you go and visit Taco in the hospital? Not once! And, in one breath, you talk about his buying you a bracelet and then you say you're going to the dance with someone else because he can't dance right now. If I were going with a boy like Taco, I'd stick by him when he was down."

Honey eyed her coolly, but her lion eyes flickered with amusement. "Yes, but unfortunately you're not going with him, are you?" she said. "In fact, Taco's told me, more than once, that it's just a great big pain to have you tagging around behind him all the time. So if I were you, I'd be a good little girl and mind my own business."

Then she swept out, leaving Fiona feeling just as miserable and confused as she had after the rodeo.

I suppose she's right, she thought. *However much I hate her, she's still right. Taco has been nice to me, but that doesn't mean Honey's ceased to exist. I must have been reading too much into the things he said to me. All the time I thought he was starting to feel something for me, he was probably only just being friendly and polite.*

She picked up her bookbag and gave a big sigh. *He probably thinks of me as a second Sherry, a little kid sister. After all, he hasn't really even kissed me again.*

"Are you taking Fiona to the luminarios, or do you want me to?" Professor West asked one night.

"I want to," Taco said. "Do you think you could drive us in? That is," he said, quickly turning to Fiona, "if you feel like going tonight."

"Is the luminarios any relative of the arroyos or bosques?" she asked.

Taco laughed. "No, it's special to Albuquerque. You'll see when we get there."

"Is it dangerous?"

"It could be, being out alone in the dark with me," he said. "You want to come anyway?"

"You bet," Fiona said.

So that evening Fiona found herself being driven toward town, not knowing whether to expect a rodeo, something to eat, or goodness knows what else.

As they approached the city, Fiona suddenly cried out in wonder. "Oh, look over there, what's that?" she said, pointing to Albuquerque, which was aglow with lights like a huge Christmas tree.

"That's luminarios," Taco said. "Or at least, that's the start of them. You could drop us off here, Dad."

They climbed down from the truck.

"Well," Taco said. "What do you think?"

"Fantastic," Fiona said. "What makes all the little lights?"

"Candles stuck in sand inside grocery bags."

"Don't the bags catch fire?"

"I never heard of it," Taco said. "Come on, let's go closer."

Fiona felt as if she were walking toward a fairyland. On every front lawn, up every front path, on every rooftop and porch, millions of lights were glowing so that each house and garden was outlined in light.

"Is this an American Christmas custom?" she asked.

"It comes from Mexico to start with," Taco said.

"It's like magic," Fiona said. "We have lights at Christmas, but nothing like this."

They walked together through the excited crowd into the middle of town. They passed a church group carrying lighted lanterns and singing carols as they walked. People were following the carol singers, linking arms and walking six abreast in the street.

Then Taco steered her away from the thickest crowds, and they found themselves alone by a beautiful fountain. It, too, was illuminated, and the lights picked up the water exploding in all directions.

"Taco, hold on a minute," Fiona begged. "You're the invalid, but I'm pooped. I don't think I shall ever be able to keep up with you."

"All right, let's sit down and rest," Taco said, going over to a nearby bench. "Listen to the silence. It doesn't feel like being in the city at all, does it?"

"I don't think I'll ever get used to the silence," Fiona said. "At home it's never—"

She didn't have time to finish her sentence. A playful wind had sprung up, and it blew a curtain of spray straight at them. She jumped up and gasped. "Taco, get up, you idiot," she yelled, watching him sit there calmly while the spray blew all over him. "You'll wreck your cast. You know you aren't supposed to get it wet."

135

Taco continued to sit there and smile. The wind dropped, and suddenly there was no sound again but the gentle splash of water.

"You want to know something?" he said at last. "I think I'm falling in love with you. Is that a bad thing?"

"No," she said, hardly daring to talk. "It's not bad at all."

He stood up and walked across to her, his footsteps echoing against the concrete. Then he leaned forward until his lips barely touched hers. "You won't tell me to go away this time, will you?" he whispered.

Her eyes were glowing just like those millions of lanterns. Fiona felt her heart pounding. "No," she said, wrapping her arms around his neck.

Chapter Eleven

Fiona lay in bed feeling warm and cozy. She yawned happily and opened her eyes. Instinctively she knew something was different. There was something about the quality of the blue light that came into her room, something about the utter quiet outside. She looked at her watch. Seven o'clock. Usually Maria and Enrique would be moving around and making a lot of noise long before seven. Then it came to her. "Of course, it's Christmas morning!"

She raised her head from the pillow and got a second surprise. It had snowed. The world outside was white as far as she could see. The familiar fences and farm machines had been turned into shapeless white mounds.

It must have snowed hard last night, she thought. *How very perfect. I don't think I've ever had a white Christmas before.*

Maria and Enrique were spending the day with their grown children, and Fiona lay there, enjoying the warmth of her bed and looking forward to a relaxed day with just Taco and Professor West. She was even looking forward to helping cook the turkey, the only thing that had to be done since Maria had been baking and cooking frantically for days and the refrigerator was bulging with casseroles, cakes, cookies, and pies.

It all worked out so perfectly, she thought, wriggling her toes with excitement. All those days of wondering and hoping and not knowing what Taco thought were over. She knew how he felt about her. She knew he cared, and it felt terrific. She also knew that she had never felt this way before. She had thought she was in love with Simon, and yet Simon had never made her legs feel all wobbly every time he looked at her. Simon was nice and kind and funny, but he didn't take over all her waking thoughts and her dreams the way Taco did. Now she had a whole Christmas Day with Taco to look forward to. They'd sit together by a big fire with the towering Christmas tree, glittering with lights and tinsel and glass balls.

Fiona heard Professor West stomping along the hall in his big boots and guiltily thought that perhaps she should get up and help with breakfast. Then the footsteps came right up to her door, and someone knocked.

"Fiona?" came the professor's voice. "Are you awake?"

Fiona pulled on her robe and went across to the door. "Merry Christmas," she said, then stopped short because he was wearing his big overcoat and scarf. "Is something wrong?" she asked.

He smiled. "No, not really. It's just, well, I hate to ask you on Christmas morning, but I'm going to need some help. You can see it snowed, and Enrique's not here, and somehow I have to get food out to the stock. I don't want Taco out there, getting his cast wet and hurting his shoulder more."

"Of course not," she said. "I don't mind at all. Just give me a few moments to get some warm clothes on."

When she was finally dressed, in so many layers that her face could hardly be seen, she met Taco in the hall.

"Hey, it's the abominable snowman," he said. "What are you all dressed up for?"

"I'm going to help your dad."

"Oh, come on, Dad," he called as his father appeared at the front door. "It's not fair to have Fiona do this. I told you I could manage all right."

"Now let's not go over this again, Taco," his father said. "Your shoulder's not strong enough for you to be out there throwing hay around."

"Well, Fiona isn't used to stuff like that."

"Listen, you," Fiona said, facing him with her hands on her hips. "I am quite capable, as you very well know, and you are not going out there and risking another visit to the hospital. Is that clear?"

"Yes, ma'am," Taco said.

Professor West laughed. "Well, that's something I never thought I'd see, someone who could actually boss my son around!"

"I don't want to boss him," Fiona said, "but it would be crazy for him to go out there."

With that, she and Professor West set off. It was snowing lightly, and their feet crunched across the soft powder that had already settled. They loaded up the truck with bales of hay, then set off across the ranch with Fiona in the back of the truck tossing out bales at intervals. The cattle stood patiently together. They were snow-covered, and their breath rose as one great cloud of steam. They lumbered hopefully toward the hay as soon as the truck was safely past them. In spite of the cold, Fiona soon found herself sweating from the effort of lifting and tossing those heavy bales. When they returned home, her cheeks were glowing pink, and there were snowflakes on her eyelashes.

"Well, that's a job done," said the professor, stomping the snow off his boots on the porch. "Now, I hope that boy's put on some coffee to warm us up."

"I did better than that," Taco called from the

kitchen, "I've got enough bacon and eggs here to feed a whole army."

"That's good because I'm starving," Fiona called back, throwing off her wet clothes. "And my hands still won't come back to life."

"Come over here, I'll make them better," Taco said. He took her hands between his and kissed her fingertips.

"Good heavens, you're a changed person," Professor West said, coming into the kitchen in the middle of the scene. "We'd better not let you go home, Fiona. You've improved my son so much recently."

"It's fine with me if she stays on," Taco said.

"But not with Sherry, who'll want her room back," Fiona said, laughing it off. "And let's not talk about going home, or I'll get depressed."

"Hey," Taco yelled suddenly, "Merry Christmas, everyone!"

After breakfast a call came through from England. Fiona found it strange to be talking to her parents. The line was so clear it was almost as if they were in the next room. Their accents sounded exaggerated and clipped after the easy New Mexican speech, and Fiona found that she was using American phrases without realizing it.

"You're becoming quite a little American," her mother noted.

The minutes of the call sped by without Fiona being able to say what she really wanted to.

Then Sherry came on the line, and Taco and his father picked up the other phone so they could all join in. Fiona thought she might feel embarrassed talking to Sherry, but when she heard her voice, she knew instantly that she could never feel embarrassed with her.

"Fiona! How are you doing?" she yelled.

"I'm fine. How are you?"

"Terrific. I'm having a wonderful English Christmas. We went to look at the lights in Oxford Street, and all the store windows were decorated just like Disneyland. Then we walked on to Trafalgar Square and saw the giant Christmas tree. Oh, and the carol singers. Tons have come to the door. One cute little boy who couldn't have been more than four or five only knew one line of 'Away in a Manger.' He just kept singing it over and over until we gave him some money. What an easy way to get rich! And we've had so much to eat, plum pudding and fruitcake and mince pies and sausage rolls. So how are you all doing? How are you getting along with that brother of mine? I didn't dare warn you about him before you left, or I knew you'd never get on the plane. Is he being an awful pest?"

"Absolutely," Fiona said on the phone extension.

"Not true," Taco interrupted. "I can't help it if she's helpless and can't even learn to drive a truck, can I?"

142

"Don't take any notice of him, Fiona," Sherry urged.

"Oh, don't worry. I don't. I just ignore him all the time," she said smoothly. Taco came down the hall and draped his arms around her shoulders. Then he started kissing the back of her neck.

"Go on with what you were saying," he said sweetly. "Don't let me distract you."

"Just wait till they get video phones," she hissed back. "Oh, no, Sherry, I wasn't talking to you. It's just your brother the pest is going to get back on the phone. Here he is." And she handed him the receiver, dodging out of the way and laughing.

Later, they opened their presents around the tree. Fiona was doubly delighted when she opened the bracelet from Taco—delighted that he had cared enough to give it to her and equally delighted that Honey, who expected it, had not gotten it.

Fiona's first American Christmas went all too quickly. Dinner was delicious, and afterward they all went outside for a snowball fight. Then, wet and laughing, they came back in, and Professor West built a fire in the fireplace. They sat in front of it, sipping hot chocolate and talking.

Later that evening Fiona was alone with Taco in the living room. She walked across to the window and looked out. The Christmas tree lights threw a warm glow onto the snow, the fire crackled in the fireplace, and a thin slice of moon hung over the hills.

Taco came to stand next to her.

"It's a perfect night," she said, turning to him.

"It certainly is," he said, bringing his lips toward hers.

"Taco, your father might come in," she whispered.

"Let him. I'm allowed to kiss my girlfriend on Christmas evening, aren't I?"

"Taco, what about Honey?" she asked.

"What about her?"

"I thought you and she were going together."

"We were."

"And?"

"We're not anymore."

"Does she know about that yet?"

"If she doesn't, she'll find out soon enough, won't she?" he said. "Let's not talk about it. I don't want anything to spoil this evening."

Fiona did not know at what stage Honey found out that she and Taco were no longer a twosome, but she had clearly heard the news by the time they went back to school. At first Fiona didn't think Honey minded very much. She seemed to be very interested in Billy Peterson, the basketball star who had taken her to the Christmas dance. She hardly looked up when Fiona and Taco went past together. But gradually Fiona came to realize that Honey might not be as unconcerned as she appeared.

It was only after a few weeks of school, when Taco had his cast off and was fully fit again, that Honey decided she wanted him back. And when he didn't come running, she started getting really nasty to Fiona. One day when Fiona was changing for gym, she heard Honey's loud voice saying, "You all know how lazy Taco always was. Never lifted a finger if he didn't have to. So why would he go out hunting if he can get all he wants right there at home!" There was a great shriek of laughter from Honey's friends, and Fiona, hating herself for blushing, stalked out of the room.

You should feel happy, she told herself. *After all, she's only acting that way because she's jealous.*

But all the pep talks in the world didn't help. For someone who was basically shy and insecure, it was torture to be whispered about and laughed at in public. She knew that all the kids didn't join in Honey's attack, but Honey and her gang always seemed to take pleasure in making her feel uncomfortable.

Rosie found her one day sitting alone on a bench. Winter was turning into spring, and the days were warm again. Fiona loved to look up at the mountains, still topped with snow that sparkled like cake frosting, and breathe in the pure air.

"All alone today?" Rosie asked, sitting down beside her.

Fiona nodded. "Taco's gone for his physiotherapy session, and Honey has taken up residence in the cafeteria, so I preferred to come out here."

Rosie nodded. "That's what I wanted to talk to you about," she said. "I wanted to warn you about Honey."

Fiona smiled. "Oh, I don't think I need warning," she said. "I get the message loud and clear. She wants Taco back, and she's mad at me. That's not hard to read."

"But I'd watch out if I were you," Rosie said, looking around as she spoke. "I mean Honey's used to getting her own way all the time. Her dad's practically a millionaire, and he'll do anything for his little girl. She hates it when someone gets in her way."

"Don't worry, Rosie," Fiona said. "She's been trying to turn everyone against me by making cheap wisecracks. I figure if I ignore her long enough, she'll stop."

"So long as she just keeps it to wisecracks," Rosie said.

Fiona looked up at her sharply. "You mean she'd try to gun me down or something?" she asked and grinned. "This may be the Wild West, but I don't believe things like that, Rosie."

"It's nothing to laugh about," Rosie said. She dropped her voice. "It's nothing obvious. But maybe something to get you out of the way or to scare you enough to go home."

"I don't think she'd do something like that, either," Fiona said.

"Well," Rosie said hesitantly, "there was this girl once, back in elementary school, who was going to get to lead the marching band in a parade, and Honey wanted to lead the band. Just a few days before the parade, the girl slipped off the parallel bars in the gym and twisted her ankle."

"Accidents happen all the time," Fiona said.

"Except that I happen to know that someone had taken the pin out of the bar before her turn," Rosie said.

"OK, so I'll be careful," Fiona said uneasily. "But I should have thought that someone like Honey could have any boy in the whole school. Why all this fuss about losing one?"

"Because she only gives up a boy when *she's* tired of him, not the other way around," Rosie said. "And she wasn't tired of Taco yet." She gave Fiona's hand a squeeze before she left.

Well, it doesn't worry me, Fiona told herself. *I'm only here a few more months, and I'm going to enjoy every minute of them. And no terrible warnings are going to keep me away from Taco, either!*

She didn't even think of the warnings again until she was riding with a truckload of students in the Wests' truck up to the mountains. Every spring Professor West led a camping weekend to an old Indian site, and eight high-school students studied the history and ecology of the area. Fiona was looking forward to it until she found out that Honey had also signed up. A whole weekend with Honey was not very appealing. Actually, Honey hadn't been too bad lately. She seemed to be really interested in Billy Peterson and to have forgotten her grudge against Fiona and Taco. Also, Rosie was going, and that pleased Fiona.

Honey smiled at Fiona as they climbed into the back of the truck. "You're going to love this," she said. "It's such fun, sleeping out and climbing up to the Indian city and everything, so much more exciting than boring old London."

Fiona nodded but didn't say anything. She was beginning to understand a little more about Honey. She felt threatened because Fiona came from London. That made her a sophisticated city girl and Honey a little country hick.

She probably thinks it's my European sophistication that took Taco away from her, Fiona thought and couldn't help smiling to herself. She was probably one of the least sophisticated girls in the entire world. But if that made Honey a bit afraid of her, she was not about to let her know the truth.

Once they reached the campsite, everyone had to get busy. Fiona found herself fetching pails of water from a spring, helping to get a fire going, and cooking the dinner.

If only my parents could see me now, she thought. *They wouldn't believe I'm their daughter.* When she thought back to her life in England, she realized how very little she used to do for herself. She thought about all those evenings with Simon, just sitting and talking and watching TV. She'd grown up a lot already, she decided as she stirred a huge pot of spaghetti sauce. She felt very good about herself, she realized, much better than she had before she left for New Mexico.

After dinner was cleared away, everyone sat around the fire while Professor West told them a bit about the history of the sky city the Indians had built; they'd be climbing to it the next day. Then they spread out their sleeping bags. As Fiona was returning from brushing her teeth, she heard voices in the darkness—one of them was Honey's.

"Oh, come on now, sweetie-pie," the voice said, floating toward her soft and low. "Let's just kiss and make up. I've been real bored without you."

"It doesn't look like you've been wasting your time," the other voice, unmistakably Taco's, answered. Fiona froze and stood in the darkness listening.

"Oh, you mean old Billy Peterson? He was

just to fill in the time until you got fed up with little what's-her-name."

"You know her name is Fiona, Honey. And I'm not fed up with her."

"You will be soon, I guarantee. After all, she *is* kind of different. All sweet and helpless and talking in that cute little English accent."

"She's not as helpless as you think," Taco said. "And she came to visit me in the hospital every day, which was more than you did."

"Darling, you know I hate the sight of blood, and hospitals depress me, so don't hold that against me," Honey coaxed. "Let's forget about that terrible hospital and start again. I mean, I'm here and you're here, and I'm ready and willing. . . ."

There was a pause, and Fiona found herself holding her breath.

"Nice try, Honey," Taco said at last, "but I don't know what it takes to get it into your head that it's over between us."

"It's not over, sweetie-pie, it's just temporarily on hold," Honey said softly. "After all, we're the same type, you and I. We belong together. They say it at all the rodeos: we make a great team. *She* doesn't belong here. She's not your type at all. You just keep your eyes open this weekend, and you'll see what a fool she makes of herself when she has to rough it in the desert."

"Now you behave yourself, Honey," Taco warned.

"Oh, I intend to," she said. "You know me, always as good as gold."

That was when Rosie's warning came back to Fiona. *I'd better be on my guard for any funny business,* she thought as she crawled into her sleeping bag.

Chapter Twelve

Next morning Fiona was about to put on her sneakers when she noticed something inside one of them, something shiny and black. Even Fiona could identify it as a scorpion. Would Honey do a terrible thing like that? Fiona knew that scorpions did like the insides of shoes, so it could have crawled in on its own, but it was strange that out of all the shoes in camp, the scorpion had selected hers. Carefully she picked up the shoe and carried it away from the sleeping bags. Then she tipped it out against a rock. The scorpion tumbled onto the soft earth and lay there unmoving. Fiona prodded it with a stick. It was plastic.

"Nice try, Honey," she said, echoing Taco's words of the night before. "I bet you wanted me to have hysterics and make a big fool of myself. Well, I think I've won the first round." She bent down, picked up the plastic scorpion, and popped it in her pocket. *I think I'll keep the evidence in case I need it,* she thought.

After breakfast the group set off on an all-day hike to the ancient Indian city. It was built at the top of a cliff on the high plateau and had been used since prehistoric times as a fortress. The Indians had defended it for hundreds of years until the Spanish blew the fortress apart with their gunpowder. There was still only one way up to it, a series of steps cut into the cliff face. Even though it was still early spring, the sun was hot, and the steps seemed incredibly steep. The others plodded up without pausing, clambering over the rocks that were still slippery from recent rains. Fiona made herself keep up with them even though her heart was hammering in her rib cage and her breath felt like fire. She was not, definitely not, going to lag behind and have Honey remind everyone that she was only a delicate little English girl.

The view from the top was breathtaking. The mountains, still capped with snow, towered majestically above the first lime-green leaves of spring. The sun burned brightly, and lizards had come out to lie on the sun-warmed rocks. Professor West led the group, pointing out where the Indians had ground their corn and baked their bread.

The Indian fort made a big impression on Fiona. She had always thought the history of

America was very short compared with that of England, but now she was learning that Indians had lived in stone houses with well-defended forts when Queen Elizabeth I ruled England and when the ordinary English people were living just as primitively. It would be interesting to point this out to her history teacher when she got home. She was sure Miss Fairbotham thought American history began with the *Mayflower*.

Fiona wandered around alone, trying to imagine how the people had lived up there years ago. She wasn't paying too much attention to where she was walking and jumped horribly when someone grabbed her arm.

"Hey, watch out, you nearly stepped on a rattlesnake!" a voice yelled behind her.

Fiona leaped back and found that her rescuer was Honey. On the path ahead of her, a fat, banded snake wriggled slowly through the sand.

"Oh, thank you, I didn't even see it," she said breathlessly.

Honey smiled back sweetly. "That's OK," she said. "A city girl like you can't be expected to know about things like rattlesnakes. But watch out in the future, now you know."

"Oh, I will," Fiona said. "Thanks again."

Honey walked away, and Fiona stood watching the snake, now lying motionless in the sun. So Honey was a nice person deep down, she told herself. She didn't mind scaring Fiona with a plastic scorpion, but she hadn't let her step on a real rattlesnake. Just then, Taco and two other boys came toward her, talking and laughing and not looking where they were going.

"Hey, watch out, there's a rattlesnake on the path up there," she called out to them.

"A rattlesnake? Where?" they called out, walking forward slowly and cautiously. The big snake heard their voices and slowly slid toward the protection of a big rock.

"You mean that?" one boy asked, starting to laugh. "That's not a rattlesnake. That's only a king snake. They wouldn't hurt a fly."

The two boys laughed, but Taco said kindly, "If I see a real rattlesnake, I'll show you. Once you've seen one, you'll be able to spot the difference in a second."

Fiona almost explained that Honey told her about the snake, but she realized that it wouldn't do much good. She'd believed Honey, so she still looked like a fool.

Round two to Honey, she thought angrily. *I wish this nonsense would stop.*

Fiona was never quite sure if there was a round three because what happened next was so hard to believe, even of Honey. It happened later that day when the group went to a lookout point where the Indians used to rain arrows down on their enemies.

"Oh, wait, you've got to see this," Honey said,

stepping aside for Fiona to take a look over the edge.

Instead Billy Peterson pushed ahead. "Hey, let me check this out," he said.

Suddenly Honey made a grab for him. "No, Billy, don't lean out there," she yelled.

That's when they found the stone at the edge of the parapet was loose.

Fiona shuddered. Honey had invited her to lean over and look. Had she known the stone was loose? Would it really have given way and pitched Fiona down into the valley? It was something she could never tell anyone, and she tried to look at it logically.

She only noticed the stone was loose when Billy stepped on it. She would have dragged me back, too, if she had seen it move, Fiona insisted to herself. But there would always be that nagging doubt, and in her mind she imagined herself tumbling over the edge and hurtling down to the rocks below.

After that, perhaps, Honey realized she had gone too far because for the rest of the day she stayed away from Fiona. That night clouds began gathering over the mountains. In the middle of the night, the group was awakened by a sudden clap of thunder, then a deluge of freezing rain.

"Fiona, come under here quick," Taco yelled, grabbing her and dragging her sleeping bag across to where he had rigged up a bit of shelter.

"Isn't this cozy," he said, sitting with his arm around her under the tarp, while the rain cascaded down all around them.

"It might be a little cozy if the ground weren't turning into a lake," Fiona pointed out. "My feet are already soaking wet."

In the end they all had to climb into the back of the truck and sit huddled together while their former campsite became a large puddle. It was not a pleasant night. Drips seemed to find their way in between the covers. Their sleeping bags all got soggy, and they were too cramped to move.

At first light Professor West suggested they pack up and go home. "There's no point in trying to do anything today," he said. "We can't get a fire going for breakfast, and I'm worried about some of the creeks filling up."

They all changed into whatever dry clothing they could find, ate cereal straight from the packages, then set off. Fiona was secretly glad. She knew she was not, and never would be, the hearty outdoor type, and she was glad she didn't have to pretend to enjoy a day in the freezing rain.

The three girls crowded into the cab of the truck with Professor West, and the boys huddled in the back. The truck slithered and lurched over dirt roads that had turned into seas of mud. Fiona remembered her famous truck ride and realized she'd been lucky it hadn't rained.

By mid-morning the rain had stopped. The sun peeked out between giant blue-black storm clouds.

"We could have stayed after all," Rosie said.

Professor West shook his head. "We don't want to risk being cut off by rising water," he said. "I don't like the look of those arroyos already. See what I mean?" he said, bringing the truck to a halt. A large dry creek they had crossed easily on their way out was now full of rushing water.

"Can we make it through that?" Rosie asked. Fiona had wanted to ask the same question and was glad that Rosie had voiced it first.

Professor West frowned. "This truck is pretty powerful," he said. "We'll just take it slowly." He inched the truck into the swirling water. The water was not deep, and they moved forward steadily. Then in mid-stream they hit a patch of soft mud. They could feel the wheels churning instead of moving forward.

"What's up, Dad?" Taco shouted from the back.

"Got bogged down in some mud," his father yelled back. "You kids had better climb down and give us a push."

"Us, too?" Honey asked. "Why don't we leave it to the big strong boys?" Fiona and Rosie laughed loudly.

"Listen, if we've got to stand up to our middles in freezing water, so do you," Taco said.

"Come on out, and I mean now," he said and laughed.

"I'm afraid you'd better get out, girls," Professor West said. "We can't have any weight we don't need in the truck."

They began to climb down, squealing as the cold water swirled around them and their shoes sank into the soft mud.

"Hey, Honey," Taco yelled. "What are you still doing in there? Get down here, too."

Honey stuck her head out of the cab. "My little weight won't make much difference, sweetie-pie, and I'm wearing expensive white Jordache jeans." She smiled to them.

"If we have to push, so do you," Rosie called.

"Oh, come on, you guys," Honey said, looking red and flustered for the first time since Fiona had met her. "I'm not ruining a good pair of jeans. You'll just have to do without me."

"Professor West, make her help," the girls pleaded.

"I think we're wasting valuable time," the professor said. "I don't want to lose my truck because of a little squabble."

"Well, we're not pushing if Honey doesn't," the boys said.

The professor looked at Honey. "Honey, I really think it would be fair if you did your share," he said. "If your clothes were too good to get wet, you shouldn't have worn them on a camp-

159

ing trip. Now let's all push before the engine gets flooded and we're stuck here permanently."

Honey climbed down. Everyone clapped loudly. The brown water swirled around her thighs as she made her way to the back of the truck. She didn't say anything, but if looks could kill, there would have been a lot of corpses floating down that river.

"OK, get ready to push. Ready, set, go!" Professor West yelled. The engine churned and whined. The truck rocked gently. Then, very slowly, they felt it inch forward until it was on firmer ground.

"Well, I can't believe you're so weak that you couldn't move this truck without me," Honey said, her face reflecting her fury. As she turned to say this, she put her foot into a pothole and went down into the brown swirling water. Everyone was helpless with laughter as they dragged her out, sputtering.

"I hope you're all satisfied now," she yelled as water dripped from her hair, making it hang like string around her face. "I might have been killed or swept away!"

"Oh, come on, Honey, it's only water," Billy said, trying to console her. "Where's your sense of humor?"

Fiona put her hand into her pocket and closed her fingers around that little plastic scorpion. *Well, I know one person who's glad Honey got what she deserved,* she thought and grinned to herself as she climbed back into the truck.

Chapter Thirteen

After the camping trip the days sped by. Fiona would look at the calendar and think, "Only two more months with Taco." Then she'd picture drab London, its long gray days and boring evenings. She'd wonder how she could ever face them again.

Sherry wrote about London fashions and rock groups, visits to famous old houses and theaters. "It's funny," Fiona said to Taco. "She sounds as if she's becoming quite an English city girl. Do you think she'll ever fit in back on the farm again?"

"Maybe we should just leave her and keep you instead," he said, drawing her close to him.

Fiona felt a horrible sense of confusion when he said things like that. She knew she had to go back. She longed to see her parents, yet she knew that part of her wouldn't feel at home in

London ever again. When she was waiting in rush-hour crowds, she would always see before her the wide-open spaces of New Mexico. When she looked at row after row of rooftops, she would always imagine the mountains and how they glowed purple at sunset. "I guess I feel like I have two homes now," she said. "And I will never really feel completely whole in either of them."

Taco smiled. "You won't like that smoggy old city after this, that's for sure."

"Oh, I don't know," she said. "There are some things that I miss badly."

"Like what?" he demanded, holding her tightly.

"Fish and chips wrapped in paper, English sausages, my favorite shows on TV."

"No problem," Taco said. "We'll just have the food flown in for you once a week and get a satellite to beam down your programs. You see, I'm not going to let you go without a fight."

"Oh, Taco," she said, brushing his lips gently with her fingertips and noticing how the skin beside his eyes crinkled when he smiled. "I wish you wouldn't make it so hard for me. Why don't you come over like your sister did if you can't bear to let me out of your sight?"

Taco wrinkled his nose. "Not me," he said. "I couldn't survive in a city. I'd choke to death on all those fumes and feel trapped by all those buildings. I like it right where I am, thank you. I just want to get college over with and farm this ranch, maybe improve the quality of the stock and develop a famous breeding herd."

Fiona sighed. "You're lucky to know what you want out of life. I don't yet, except that now I've started to travel, I know I've got to see some more of the world. Maybe I'll become an airline flight attendant. Then I can pop in to visit during my stopovers in New Mexico!"

"No, I know those flight attendants, a man in every airport," he said. "I wouldn't want to share you."

"Hey," she said, breaking away, "I don't know why we're talking like this. It's depressing. We both know I've got to go soon, so let's just enjoy the time we've got, OK?"

"Very wise," he said. "And I've got a great way to enjoy the present, starting right now." His lips touched hers in a warm, gentle kiss.

With the coming of spring, flowers burst into bloom all over the scrub land and desert. The yuccas shot up like great white candles, and the new grass delighted the cattle.

On the ranch things were very busy. It was the time for the yearly roundup and branding of the new calves. Fiona went along to watch. She didn't volunteer to help, but watched from the safety of the truck. She knew that she wasn't the kind of rider who could make her mount weave in and out of all those frightened animals. Taco was back in the saddle again, his shoulder as good as new, and Fiona admired the way he could single out one calf from a group of cows, making his horse change direction with no apparent effort. *He really wouldn't belong anywhere but here,* she thought sadly.

The branding of the calves scared her. Those terrified bellows and the smell of scorching flesh were hard to accept.

"Isn't it terribly cruel?" she asked Taco.

"Oh, they've got tough hides. They don't feel a thing," he said. "They're just scared, that's why they call for their mothers. And if we didn't catch them and brand them, our neighbors would end up with half our herd each year."

But Fiona was still not convinced. That was another difference between Taco and her. He was practical while she was much more senti-mental. And yet, Taco was a strange mixture of practical and sentimental, as their final trip together proved.

The school year had come to an end with all sorts of exciting happenings. Fiona had sung in a concert, been to Taco's graduation, and gone to lots of parties. Finally there had been a wonderful open-air dance. Fiona's days in New Mexico were now numbered.

One day she overheard Taco and his father discussing a trip. They passed together beside her open window, and it sounded from Professor West's voice as if he was not in favor of the idea.

"But, Dad," Taco was saying, "think what a special experience it would be for her, something she could never see anyplace else in the world."

"I know, Taco, but I feel responsible for her. Can I trust you?" Then they passed out of earshot.

Fiona forgot all about the conversation, she was so busy with last-minute shopping for presents and with all the other things she had not managed to cram into a school year.

She was trying very hard not to think about going home and life without Taco, but a tiny part of her could not help but feel excited at the thought of returning to England. She longed to share her photos with her parents and friends, to say, "This was the day we climbed a mountain; this was the day our truck got stuck in the river. . . ." She was looking forward to being able to walk to a corner store to buy English candy bars or fish and chips.

One night toward the end of June Fiona had a dream about Taco. He was beside her, whispering wonderful things. "Fiona," he was saying, "Fiona, wake up." Then he kissed her very gently on her cheek.

"Taco?" she murmured. Then she opened her eyes. Taco really *was* sitting on her bed, smiling down at her.

"Gee, you sleep soundly," he said, grinning. "I thought I was never going to be able to wake you."

"Taco, what are you doing in here, it's the middle of the night!" Fiona said uneasily.

"It's not the middle of the night, it's three-thirty in the morning," Taco said.

"But what would your father say if he found you in my room?" Fiona asked.

Taco laughed. "He gave me permission. And you don't have to worry, I only came to wake you up. We're going on a special trip."

"At three-thirty in the morning?" Fiona asked. She shivered in the early chill and pulled her covers more firmly around her.

"It's a special trip. We have to get somewhere by sunrise," Taco said, grabbing her arm. "Now will you get up!"

"Get where by sunrise?" she asked stubbornly.

"It's a secret, and we'll miss it if you don't hurry," he said firmly. "Now am I going to have to drag you to the truck in your nightgown, or will you get up and get ready!"

"I think you're crazy," she said, climbing out of bed. "But I'm not about to turn down a chance to go somewhere with you."

"I'll pour some coffee," he said, going toward the door. Then he added, "And bring it out to the truck. We have a long way to drive."

Fiona felt only half-awake as she walked to

166

the truck. The sky above was still heavy with stars.

"Look at the sky," she whispered to Taco. "Those stars seem so close, I feel I could almost reach out and grab one."

"You won't see stars like that in smoggy old England," he said, helping her climb into the cab.

"No depressing talk allowed," she said.

"You're right," he agreed. "I was just thinking that this is probably the last time we'll be alone together. Totally alone, I mean."

She nodded and didn't say any more. They drove southeast, heading into the desert. Through the darkness Fiona could make out the ghostly shapes of giant cactuses beside the road, looking like weird hitchhikers waiting for rides. "Why won't you tell me where we're going?" she asked at length. "I hope it's not more wild horses."

"It's not more wild horses, and you are too curious," he said.

"So you won't tell me," she said in a thick European accent. "We have ways of making you talk."

"Oh, yeah?"

"First, the death by a thousand kisses."

"I could die from worse."

"You mean you're still not going to tell me? You are a beast! How do you know if I'll like it?"

"You'll like it."

After they had been driving for about an hour,

Taco swung the truck off the paved road onto a trail that Fiona could barely see in the darkness. "I hope you don't intend to abandon me in the desert," she said.

Taco gave her a wicked grin. "How did you guess?" he said. "I decided I want my bracelet back."

Fiona fondled the cool silver band on her wrist. "I shall wear this every day in England," she said, "even though it is forbidden with my school uniform. I shall wear it under my shirt cuff so no one will know it's there, and whenever I get depressed, I shall touch it and think of you."

"No depressing talk allowed, you said it yourself," Taco said. "Anyway, I need to concentrate from now on, or I'll miss the trail, and then we really will wind up lost in the desert."

Fiona peered ahead into the darkness. She marveled at how Taco could see a trail at all. The desert floor was flat as far as the headlights penetrated. The truck bumped over small rocks, and thorny bushes screeched along the sides of the truck. At last Fiona could make out a line of cliffs ahead. There was a hint of light in the sky. The cliffs came closer and closer until finally Taco brought the truck to a halt close to the black wall.

"From now on it's on foot," he said.

The wind was whistling through the crags as they climbed down from the cab. Taco shone a flashlight ahead of them. "Watch your step," he said. "It's kind of steep at the beginning."

They followed a winding trail that led upward between the cliffs.

It was very spooky in the darkness of the cliffs. The sound of their footsteps was magnified as if two giants were walking or as if someone large were walking behind them. Fiona turned around more than once. Even their breathing sounded loud.

"Here we are," Taco said at last.

In the gray half light, Fiona could see that they were in a narrow valley between tall cliffs.

"What am I supposed to see at this time of night?" Fiona asked.

"Be patient," Taco said. "It's not long now."

"Where are we?" Fiona asked. She realized that they were speaking in whispers, as if the place were somehow magical.

"This is an old Indian site," Taco said. "Look." He shone his flashlight on the cliffs, and Fiona gasped.

"Oh, there are carvings," she said. She shivered in spite of herself.

"What's the matter?" Taco asked.

"I was thinking about the Indians," she said. "Do you think there are ghosts here?"

"No, this was a holy place. You don't have to be afraid," he said. "Come and stand over here by me. This is what I wanted to show you."

169

Fiona stood beside him at the base of the cliff.

"Now see the signs on the rock," he told her.

She looked obediently. "These arrows, you mean?"

"Right, now follow this arrow upward with your eyes."

"To that crack in the rocks?"

"Right."

"Then what?"

"Then we wait."

"What for?"

"Shut up and keep watching."

Fiona stared at the crack in the rocks and wondered what she should be looking at. Then suddenly a blinding light came through the crack, looking like a star imprisoned in stone.

"What is it?" Fiona asked, afraid. She could easily believe in ghosts of old Indian warriors coming down to earth.

"It's the rising sun," Taco whispered, his voice a little shaky. "Do you know what day it is?"

"It's—" Fiona checked her watch. "It's June twenty-first."

"Summer solstice," he said. "You're looking at a calendar. The sun only shines through this crack as it rises on the solstice."

"You mean the Indians thought that out long ago?"

"Very long ago. My father thinks the designs on the rock are almost two thousand years old."

Fiona looked in wonder. It *was* almost magical—the pinpoint of brilliant light fell exactly on the old carvings, just as it should. And it had been worked out by people who lived when England was primitive, also.

Taco touched Fiona's hand. "I just wanted you to know that we're not totally primitive over here and that we have a history, too."

"You're proud of it, aren't you?" she asked, turning to him.

"Very," he said. "I wanted you to understand why I could never live in Europe."

They stood staring at the crack for a few more minutes.

Finally Fiona said, "Oh, it's gone." The bright light had vanished from the crack, and the valley was again plunged into gloom.

"It only lasts about ten minutes," he said. "You are one of the few people who has ever seen it. My father discovered it about eight years ago, and so far only a handful of scholars has been allowed to come here. Come on, let's go and cook some breakfast. I'm starving."

Afterward, when they were back in the truck, Fiona said, "Taco, would you kiss me goodbye now? I don't want to at the airport when everyone is watching."

"Why now? You're not leaving for two days yet."

Fiona gave a deep sigh. "I know. And we'll

171

have time alone together before I leave, but somehow it just seems right to say goodbye here."

"Hey, it's not the end of the world," he said, noticing that she was very near to tears. "There are planes. We can see each other over vacations."

She shook her head. "No, I want to say goodbye now and remember everything just as perfectly as it is today. It's better like this; I don't belong in your world, and you wouldn't belong in mine."

He smiled into her eyes as he took her in his arms. "I bet those English boys don't know how to kiss like me," he said.

Fiona was reminded sharply that Simon had said the same thing just before she left. *Simon?* she thought. *Can I ever fall in love with someone like Simon again?*

Then she didn't think any more as the magic of Taco's kiss swept over her. Afterward they drove home in silence, sitting very close together.

Chapter Fourteen

Sherry arrived home a day before Fiona was due to leave. She came bursting into the house like a miniature tornado, talking nonstop and hugging Taco, Maria, and Enrique. Professor West, who had met her at the airport, stood behind her smiling.

"Oh, look at you, you're wonderful," Sherry said to everyone in general. "You haven't changed at all. Quick, Maria, cook me up a batch of pancakes. I'll die if I don't have some syrup soon, oh, and coffee for breakfast and some juicy ribs and a good hamburger, all the things I've longed for. And just to get on a horse and ride and ride. In England you can't just escape. All the land belongs to someone, and there are fences and hedges everywhere."

Fiona had tactfully stayed in her room while Sherry arrived so that she had a chance to say hello to everyone, but now she heard Sherry calling out, "Where's Fiona? What have you done with her, Taco? I hope you didn't let her ride Princess. I hope you were nice to her."

Fiona came into the kitchen, and Sherry looked at her in surprise. "Wowee, have you changed," she said. "Your mom won't recognize you."

"Have I? I didn't notice," Fiona said, surprised.

"You sure have. You look so tanned and healthy. When I first met you, you looked like a puff of wind would blow you away. Don't you think she's changed, Taco?"

"A little," he said.

"By the way, Fiona, how was this terrible brother of mine?"

Taco and Fiona exchanged a glance above Sherry's head. A secret smile flashed between them.

"He wasn't too bad," Fiona said.

"Yeah, but I had to kick her occasionally," Taco answered.

Sherry looked from one to the other. "Oh," she said as she began to understand. "So it's like that, is it?"

"Yes," Taco answered, going over to Fiona and putting an arm around her.

"Well," Sherry said, sounding amazed, "who would have thought it."

Later, when Sherry and Fiona were alone together, Sherry said casually, "I'm real glad about you and Taco. I was feeling awfully guilty about Simon and me. I really didn't mean it to happen, it just—sort of happened. I guess he was missing you, and I was lonely and—"

"It's OK, Sherry," Fiona cut in. "You don't have to apologize to me. Everything turned out very well, didn't it? And how is Simon, anyway?"

Sherry grinned. "He'll survive. We had a fond farewell scene, and he begged me to stay, but I guess he'll get over it. He's awfully sweet, but to tell you the truth, he's a bit of a stick-in-the-mud. I mean, I can't spend my whole life doing homework and watching TV."

Fiona smiled. "I know what you mean," she said. "Well, faithful old Richie is still waiting for you if you want him. He talked about you every time I saw him in school."

"Really?" Sherry looked pleased. "You know, sometimes in London I almost got around to writing him. I decided it must be an acute case of homesickness, and I stopped myself just in time. But it will be good to see all the gang again. How's Honey, by the way?"

"Honey?" Fiona said and smiled. "She fell down in the mud in her white jeans, and she hasn't spoken to Taco or me since, but it's a long story. Get Taco to tell you when I'm gone."

Sherry wrinkled her nose, looking very much like her brother. "He's going to be terrible to live with when you go. You must know how he sulks."

"I expect I'll be pretty terrible, too," Fiona agreed. "But I must go home. We're just going to have to get used to doing without each other."

Sherry couldn't stay in a somber mood for long. "Well, I've got to unpack," she said, grabbing Fiona and dragging her with her. "Come and see the darling clothes I've bought. You won't believe what's in fashion now. I have the cutest minidress, and I've got all the latest records. Don't you just love Urban Slime?"

"What is it?" Fiona asked cautiously.

Sherry let out a big giggle. "It's a new group. They're very big in London. Haven't they gotten over here yet?"

"Not that I know of," Fiona said, feeling like a country bumpkin. "It's funny, I haven't thought about clothes or records or movies all year. There's been so much to do."

"I know," Sherry said. "Feeding stupid cows, stupid chickens, and stupid horses. I've been dreading it after that easy life in England."

"I kind of enjoyed it," Fiona said. "It was nice to feel useful. I think I'll get a job when I'm home again. And I ought to keep up my riding. I was just wasting my life before."

"I went riding once," Sherry said, "but they make you sit on a funny little saddle, and you can only walk in a long line with other horses, and all the other riders had velvet caps on with matching jackets and riding breeches. They stared at my jeans as if I were a bug on the sidewalk. I didn't go again."

That's right, Fiona thought sadly. *People do that in England. You have to match everyone else or they stare at you. Over here you can be yourself. Perhaps I will come back one day after all. . . .*

The next morning they drove to the airport. It was a perfect day. The sky was a deep blue, and the yuccas still bloomed over all the hillsides.

"Come back and see us, won't you?" Enrique called as Fiona climbed into the truck.

"Take care, little one," Maria said, wiping her eyes.

Fiona turned to look back at the ranch house and the wide fields beyond. Then she sighed and turned her eyes firmly forward. Taco reached across and took her hand. Fiona swallowed back the tears as the truck bounced down the road. Professor West, at the wheel, chatted happily as if it were just an ordinary day and not one on which the world was to end. Fiona and Taco said nothing.

When they got to the airport, they parked the truck, then walked across the echoing terminal. Fiona felt as if she were in a trance as she handed the clerk her ticket, gave him her luggage, and walked to the gate.

"Well, goodbye, Fiona, it was lovely having you with us," Professor West said, holding out his hand to her. "I think you've gained a lot from this year, more than Sherry did. All she seems to have learned are the names of hundreds of rock groups. Tell your parents you've turned into a great little horsewoman—and don't forget us."

What a dumb thing to say, Fiona thought as she took his hand. *As if I could ever forget.*

The loudspeaker called her flight for boarding. Fiona turned to Taco. "Goodbye," she said. "Don't go roping any mustangs when I'm not there."

He smiled, his wonderful crinkle-eyed smile. "And don't go falling into any more prickly pears," he said lightly, "in case you meet any in London, that is."

"I won't. Goodbye. . . ." She turned away and hurried toward the plane. In the doorway she looked back once more through the glass.

Taco's eyes met hers. "I love you," he mouthed.

"I love you, too," she mouthed back, not caring who could see. Then she ran to the plane.

It was not long before the plane took off. It sped down the runway and lifted effortlessly into the air. Down below the white airport buildings looked like dolls' houses. She caught a glimpse of the red truck, still parked in its space. Although no one below could see, she waved. She went on waving until the truck was just an unidentifiable speck.

* * *

178

Fiona had been home a few days before she saw Simon. She met him, of all places, in the greengrocer's shop, where she had just bought two pounds of potatoes and forgotten that in England she had to bring her own bag. "Well, I can't carry them home in my pockets," she was saying, feeling very annoyed with the clerk. "You must have a bag in the store."

"I can wrap them in a bit of newspaper, love," the clerk said. "New here, are you?"

"I'll carry them for her. Put them in this basket," said a voice behind her, and it was Simon.

"Welcome home," he said shyly. "I thought I saw you. I've been following you down the street."

"Hello, Simon," she said. "Thanks for rescuing my potatoes."

"I'll walk you home, if I may," he said, holding the basket steadily as the clerk tipped the potatoes in it.

"OK," she said.

He grinned. "Very Americanized," he said. "But I shall be able to understand you because I got used to talking to Sherry."

"So I hear," she said with a cheeky grin.

He blushed and looked embarrassed. "Yes, well, I don't quite know what to say about that," he said.

Fiona smiled. *I wonder if Taco ever blushed,* she thought. Out loud she said, "Don't feel bad,

I understand perfectly. The Americans do seem to have an irresistible charm, don't they?"

"You found that out, too?"

"Very much so."

"Oh?" he looked inquiringly.

"I'll tell you all about it sometime," she said, "but not now."

They crossed the street together. Fiona stayed close to Simon, feeling threatened by the way in which people hurried along and the traffic whizzed by on the wrong side.

"She is a great girl, Sherry," Simon said, "but can she talk! I mean, she never stops. To tell you the truth, Fiona, I'm sort of glad the year's over. I feel like a bit of peace and quiet."

Fiona smiled again. Sherry and Simon, she thought, attracted to each other because they were so different. But it wasn't meant to last. What about Taco and her? She made a great mental effort and switched off thoughts of Taco.

"You've changed a lot," Simon said.

"How?"

"I don't know. You seem much more grown up, more sure of yourself. And you look so revoltingly healthy."

"It comes from throwing around bales of hay at six in the morning."

"How horrible."

"No, it was quite fun, actually."

They reached her house. "I say, Fiona," he began. "Would you—I mean, shall we—can I still come round and visit sometimes, perhaps go to a movie with you?"

"So long as it's just friends, Simon," she said. "I don't feel ready for anything more than that. I won't for a long while."

"Just friends, I promise you," he said.

"In that case, I could use a friend right now," she said.

He smiled. "I've missed you," he said.

Fiona smiled. "You know what, Simon? It's nice to be home."

Sherry's letter arrived a few days later.

Dear Fiona,

I hope by now you will have made your peace with Simon. I felt so guilty when I was in England, but now I'm back I can look at it all differently. It was like a vacation romance, that's all. I know you and Taco had more than that. I can tell the real thing when I see it! Richie's been calling daily, and you know what? He's much cuter than I remembered and more interesting, too. He's built this terrific customized sports car, and we zoom around the countryside in it!

Taco's moping around the house like a bear with a sore head. I guess it will take him awhile to get over you. He keeps getting out the atlas and poring over maps of England, and he's talking of getting a weekend job down at the riding stables—so don't be surprised if he shows up on your doorstep one day.

But in a way I hope he doesn't. He couldn't be happy anywhere but here, and we've all got a lot of changing to do in the next few years. Sometimes it only spoils it to see someone you've loved again.

I'm trying to look at it this way—it was fun to travel and to date boys from a different sort of life, but that was all part of growing up. Next year we'll be different people again, and who knows where we'll end up? But it was fun, wasn't it? And worth it?

Fiona put the letter down. "Oh, yes," she said, gazing out of the window over the gray rooftops to where a hint of green hill could be seen.

"It was worth it. Every moment."

Sweet Dreams ®

We hope you enjoyed reading this book. All the titles currently available in the Sweet Dreams series are listed on the next two pages. Ask for them in your local bookshop or newsagent. Two new titles are published each month.

If you would like to know more about Sweet Dreams, or if you have difficulty obtaining any of the books locally, or if you would like to tell us what you think of the series, write to:—

<u>United Kingdom</u>
Kim Prior,
Corgi Books,
Century House,
61-63 Uxbridge Road,
London W5 5SA,
England

<u>Australia</u>
Sally Porter,
Corgi and
Bantam Books,
26 Harley Crescent,
Condell Park 220,
N.S.W., Australia

20323	1	P.S. I LOVE YOU (1)	Barbara Conklin
20325	8	THE POPULARITY PLAN (2)	Rosemary Vernon
20327	4	LAURIE'S SONG (3)	Suzanne Rand
20328	2	PRINCESS AMY (4)	Melinda Pollowitz
20326	6	LITTLE SISTER (5)	Yvonne Greene
20324	X	CALIFORNIA GIRL (6)	Janet Quin-Harkin
20604	4	GREEN EYES (7)	Suzanne Rand
20601	X	THE THOROUGHBRED (8)	Joanna Campbell
20744	X	COVER GIRL (9)	Yvonne Greene
20745	8	LOVE MATCH (10)	Janet Quin-Harkin
20787	3	THE PROBLEM WITH LOVE (11)	Rosemary Vernon
20788	1	NIGHT OF THE PROM (12)	Debra Spector
17779	6	THE SUMMER JENNY FELL IN LOVE (13)	Barbara Conklin
17780	X	DANCE OF LOVE (14)	Jocelyn Saal
17781	8	THINKING OF YOU (15)	Jeanette Nobile
17782	6	HOW DO YOU SAY GOODBYE? (16)	Margaret Burman
17783	4	ASK ANNIE (17)	Suzanne Rand
17784	2	TEN BOY SUMMER (18)	Janet Quin-Harkin
17791	5	LOVE SONG (19)	Anne Park
17792	3	THE POPULARITY SUMMER (20)	Rosemary Vernon
17793	1	ALL'S FAIR IN LOVE (21)	Jeanne Andrews
17794	X	SECRET IDENTITY (22)	Joanna Campbell
17797	4	FALLING IN LOVE AGAIN (23)	Barbara Conklin
17800	8	THE TROUBLE WITH CHARLIE (24)	Joan Lowery Nixon
17795	8	HER SECRET SELF (25)	Rhondi Vilott
17796	6	IT MUST BE MAGIC (26)	Marian Woodruff
17798	2	TOO YOUNG FOR LOVE (27)	Gailanne Maravel
17801	6	TRUSTING HEARTS (28)	Jocelyn Saal
17813	X	NEVER LOVE A COWBOY (29)	Jesse Dukore
17814	8	LITTLE WHITE LIES (30)	Lois I. Fisher
17839	3	TOO CLOSE FOR COMFORT (31)	Debra Spector
17840	7	DAYDREAMER (32)	Janet Quin-Harkin
17841	5	DEAR AMANDA (33)	Rosemary Vernon
17842	3	COUNTRY GIRL (34)	Melinda Pollowitz
17843	1	FORBIDDEN LOVE (35)	Marian Woodruff
17844	X	SUMMER DREAMS (36)	Barbara Conklin
17846	6	PORTRAIT OF LOVE (37)	Jeanette Nobile
17847	4	RUNNING MATES (38)	Jocelyn Saal
17848	2	FIRST LOVE (39)	Debra Spector
17849	0	SECRETS (40)	Anna Aaron

17850 4	THE TRUTH ABOUT ME AND BOBBY V (41)	Janetta Johns
17851 2	THE PERFECT MATCH (42)	Marian Woodruff
17850 2	TENDER LOVING CARE (43)	Anne Park
17853 9	LONG DISTANCE LOVE (44)	Jesse Dukore
17069 4	DREAM PROM (45)	Margaret Burman
17070 8	ON THIN ICE (46)	Jocelyn Saal
17071 6	TE AMO MEANS I LOVE YOU (47)	Deborah Kent
17072 4	DIAL L FOR LOVE (48)	Marian Woodruff
17073 2	TOO MUCH TO LOSE (49)	Suzanne Rand
17074 0	LIGHTS, CAMERA, LOVE (50)	Gailanne Maravel
17075 9	MAGIC MOMENTS (51)	Debra Spector
17076 7	LOVE NOTES (52)	Joanna Campbell
17087 2	GHOST OF A CHANCE (53)	Janet Quin-Harkin
17088 0	I CAN'T FORGET YOU (54)	Lois I. Fisher
17089 9	SPOTLIGHT ON LOVE (55)	Nancy Pines
17090 2	CAMPFIRE NIGHTS (56)	Dale Cowan
17871 7	ON HER OWN (57)	Suzanne Rand
17872 5	RHYTHM OF LOVE (58)	Stephanie Foster
17873 3	PLEASE SAY YES (59)	Alice Owen Crawford
17874 1	SUMMER BREEZES (60)	Susan Blake
17876 8	JUST LIKE THE MOVIES (62)	Suzanne Rand

NON-FICTION TITLES

17859 8	THE SWEET DREAMS BEAUTIFUL HAIR BOOK	Courtney Dewitt
17838 5	THE LOVE BOOK	Deidre Laiken and Alan Schneider
17845 8	THE BODY BOOK	Deidre Laiken and Alan Schneider
17077 5	HOW TO TALK TO BOYS AND OTHER IMPORTANT PEOPLE	Catherine Winters

All's fair in love and war . . .

PLEASE SAY YES

Alice Owen Crawford

Marley couldn't be happier when shy, handsome Jeff finally asks her out. But disaster strikes when the Riverport High basketball team is left a large sum of money. The boys' team insists the money was meant for them along; the girls' team thinks that it should be shared.

The school is split right down the middle – boys on one side, girls on the other. To force the issue, the girls declare a 'romantic freeze'. No dates, no kissing, no hand-holding until the boys give in.

Marley's new romance seems doomed, unless the two opposing camps can reach a compromise – and soon!

Nina would do almost anything for Scott . . .

LITTLE WHITE LIES

Lois I. Fisher

Everyone says Nina has a good imagination, a gift for telling stories. In fact, it's one of her stories that attracts Scott to her. He's one of the Daltonites, the most sophisticated clique in the school. Nina can't believe she's dating him!

But Nina soon finds that the Daltonites don't welcome outsiders. So she impresses Scott's friends with her stories. It's so easy: a little exaggeration here, a white lie there.

I'm doing this for Scott, she thinks. But her lies finally start to catch up with her, and Nina's afraid of losing Scott forever.